BLAST TO OBLIVION

Fifteen years in a penitentiary had warped his mind, and Zach Skann came to Denver toting a deadly 12-gauge Greener shotgun . . . His victim, mines investor Ryan Bennett, had been responsible for his incarceration and his comrades' hangings. Subsequently, gun-for-hire Joshua Dillard was summoned by Bennett's sister Flora to seek the truth about her brother's murder. To clear up the accusations and trickery, Joshua rode to a mining-town hell-hole. There the trail of inquiry became a trail of more blood!

Books by Chap O'Keefe
in the Linford Western Library:

GUNSMOKE NIGHT
THE GUNMAN AND THE ACTRESS
THE REBEL AND THE HEIRESS
MISFIT LIL GETS EVEN
MISFIT LIL FIGHTS BACK
PEACE AT ANY PRICE
MISFIT LIL HIDES OUT
A GUNFIGHT TOO MANY
MISFIT LIL CLEANS UP

CHAP O'KEEFE

BLAST TO OBLIVION

Complete and Unabridged

LINFORD
Leicester

First published in Great Britain in 2009 by
Robert Hale Limited
London

First Linford Edition
published 2010
by arrangement with
Robert Hale Limited
London

British Library CIP Data

O'Keefe, Chap.
  Blast to oblivion. - -
  (Linford western library)
  1. Western stories.
  2. Large type books.
  I. Title II. Series
  823.9'14–dc22

  ISBN 978–1–84782–966–5

Published by
F. A. Thorpe (Publishing)
Anstey, Leicestershire

Set by Words & Graphics Ltd.
Anstey, Leicestershire
Printed and bound in Great Britain by
T. J. International Ltd., Padstow, Cornwall

This book is printed on acid-free paper

'The old wheel turns, and the same spoke comes up. It's all been done before, and will be again.'

The Valley of Fear
Sir Arthur Conan Doyle

1

The Shotgun Killing

The lone stranger in the dirty grey topcoat had murder on his mind. It had festered there fifteen years, poisoning his very soul. He didn't think of it as murder. He thought of it as retribution.

Tonight was the night! His triumph was close!

He stopped a spell in Holladay Street, sometimes called The Row and the heart of the red-light district with every house on it a fancy house. But its attractions didn't keep him long despite his lengthy, forced abstinence from the pleasures of female company.

'My, my, mister — that was fast.' Not that it mattered, but the girl at Hattie Soames's place felt she'd short-changed him.

For the sake of propriety and strict

relevance, most of the unfortunate's other thoughts can be left unreported. But when her glowering visitor was quickly gone, heading off into the early night, leaving her to shrug and wonder, she wished he could have been . . . well, less ripe. She was also to remember later the fearsome gun he'd carried with him in lieu of baggage.

The man strode south-east, crossing Larimer, Lawrence and several other streets till he came to Broadway and the beginnings of the subdivision already called Capitol Hill.

Full dark had come early that night in Denver with black thunderheads building and blotting out the spangle of stardrift over the great new stone mansions erected here and there for the swells.

The burgeoning city sat isolated more than 600 miles from any counterpart and an exact mile above sea level. In this section, in the light of a fine day, any visitor might have caught his breath at the bold foothills and towering

14,000-foot peaks of the Rocky Mountains to the west; the barren sprawl of never-ending high desert terrain to the east.

But tonight there was no such sightseer to view the grandeur — only the burly fellow who pressed on with a mite unsteady gait against a mounting wind along the open streets.

His attire was out of place for a neighbourhood which favoured well-pressed suits of imported worsted, black silk top hats and boots of polished cordovan leather. He wore his dirty old coat over a grimy red shirt and canvas work pants, had scuffed, clay-stained boots, and a sweat-stained hat with dark tufts of unruly hair poking from under the band. He reeked of cheap liquor and, as the bride of the multitudes had noted, the unwashed parts of his body.

He also carried a 12-gauge, double-barrelled shotgun, loaded with buckshot.

It was a genuine, patented Greener — the Treble Wedge-Fast Hammerless Gun, also known as the Facile Princeps.

The carrier knew no Latin but he understood this translated as 'easily the first' and that it was descriptive of the most murderous weapon he could have. The gun was cocked by the dropping of the barrels.

His restless, mean eyes surveyed the dotted, multistorey piles of the new rich with resentment.

Eventually, he halted before a castle-like, Romanesque residence that stood well apart from the next nearest residence, clad with smooth brown sandstone. Its silhouette was festooned with turrets and towers and liberally punctuated with glazed windows where bright lamps leaked their light around the edges of thick drapes.

Since Colorado's early gold rush days had been succeeded by the territory's statehood in 1876 and the silver age had dawned, several imposing residences had been erected in this quarter, close to the ten acres donated by a city father for a state capitol building. Henry C. Brown, twentysome years previously a mere carpenter from Ohio, was growing ever richer from the development of surrounding real estate. Prime sites were selling to mining entrepreneurs, merchants and other bigshots who wanted handsome homes nearby the state's future headquarters.

From within the elaborate mansion approached by the late-night shotgun-toter could be heard the melodious notes of a well-tuned piano, played adagio. A woman's voice sang softly, meltingly sweet.

Beautiful dreamer, wake unto me,
Starlight and dewdrops are waiting
for thee;
Sounds of the rude world heard in
the day,
Lull'd by the moonlight have all
pass'd away!

The prowler scowled and bit back the bitter oath that took shape on his lips. Reason prevailed. Vengeance was close to being his, it would be foolish now to spoil the victory. He shook the fearsome shotgun in lieu of a shouted denial of the sentimental song.

He entered the house's grounds and worked his way around to the closed and latched screen door of the darkened kitchen.

The shotgun was carefully propped beside the door. He got to work forcing the latches and locks, reflecting the while on what he'd been told by a crooked gunsmith who'd been a fellow prisoner in the penitentiary.

Greener scatterguns had performed best at recent gun trials in London and Chicago. The company advertised that its guns would shoot a closer pattern than any other manufacturer's. A Greener 12-gauge was warranted to shoot an average pattern of 210 when others could average only 127. Shot patterns showed how widely the pellets were dispersed at a given distance once they were released.

Not being a whiz at mental arithmetic, the man forcing an entry to the hilltop mansion reckoned 210 sounded twice as damaging as 127. That would be *bloody* good . . .

With a grunt of satisfaction he pushed back the kitchen door, took up his weapon and vanished into the deeper shadows of the interior.

The sounds of the unseen singer and the piano-playing drifted louder through the open door:

Beautiful dreamer, queen of my song,
List while I woo thee with soft melody;
Gone are the cares of life's busy throng,
Beautiful dreamer, awake unto me!
Beautiful dreamer, awake —

The song ended abruptly in a startled woman's scream and a man's alarmed and angry protest. This was followed by the muffled sounds of struggle and toppled furniture. Then came the boom of a shotgun, muffled by the stone of the house's solid walls. It could have been mistaken for a first clap of approaching thunder.

Had anyone been passing close, they would have heard a man cry, 'He's done for! Oh, Christ, what a thing to happen!' The woman who'd sung sobbed once or twice before quickly falling silent. Frantic activity ensued; urgent conversation and rapid footsteps went through the house and up and down stairs.

But long minutes elapsed — a full fifteen of them — before the alien figure in tattered coat and sweat-stained hat emerged from the back of the house and hurried away, swinging the Greener scattergun, coat-tails flapping in the wind and the first big spots of rain.

★ ★ ★

Women had worried about their menfolk since time immemorial: fathers, brothers, husbands, sons. In Joshua Dillard's experience as a Pinkerton

Detective Agency operative and later a general troubleshooter on his own account, their concern was often unnecessary. Joshua's territory comprised the Frontier West, which was the kind of place that attracted the bold and self-sufficient man and quickly gave he who was neither the message that he was best advised to light out, promptly and headlong, for safer haunts.

But Joshua did not turn a blind eye to the brief letter he received from Flora Bennett. Miss Bennett wanted to meet with him to discuss her brother at the sumptuous downtown hotel where she was a guest.

Joshua had several good reasons to accept the invitation.

The brother, Ryan Bennett, was already dead. His demise some six months previous, the victim of a gruesome shotgun murder, had been reported by all four Denver newspapers in avid, scandalized detail.

Rye Bennett had shared Joshua's 'ex-Pink' background, though it had been in another part of the country and his later life had led him to a very different, very prosperous scene at complete variance with Joshua's own, habitually impoverished circumstances.

Flora Bennett had told him in her letter that she'd known Joshua's wife before his marriage to her . . . and so before, Joshua was inevitably reminded, the never-to-be-forgotten incident in San Antonio, Texas. On a day of gunsmoke and blood, an outlaw gang had blown away the light of his life, robbing him of wife and happiness, sowing the seed of a hatred of crime that made him capable of killing owlhoots and villains without compunction — a justice-seeker, in fact, all too implacable and unsubtle for the reasoning Pinkertons.

Lastly, Joshua was down on his financial luck, as usual, and already in Denver after attending the wedding of Emily Greatheart, a grateful young woman he'd once rescued from the brink of death in Arizona. His client in that case had been Emily's crippled father who'd clung on to life in Denver only until he'd known she was safe. Though the chain of events had brought Joshua no monetary reward, he now counted plucky Emily as a friend and had been pleased by the chance to check her life was back on an even keel.

Of course, Flora Bennett might be a whimpering, simpering fool with a bee in her bonnet, but she did write a brisk, businesslike, no-nonsense letter which piqued his curiosity. Thus, after some reflective consideration of the tears and regrets of his life and fate's crazy games, Joshua hied himself to the hotel's marble-floored and dignified halls at the appointed time.

The smell of money was tantalizing and everywhere. He was shown into a private lounge that went under the name of the Grand Salon. The woman waiting for him rose from a Windsor armchair with a high comb back and a red velvet cushion on the seat. The chair, Joshua noted, was one of a pair

11

set either side of a small table under a crystal chandelier suspended from an ornamentally plastered ceiling.

At this hour of the early afternoon, city society was about its business, even if that was only a garden party for the local bigwigs. Flora Bennett was the Grand Salon's only occupant. She was of more than medium height and looked every inch a thorough-bred, a woman to make a man's mouth dry and his blood pump faster.

She favoured him with a gracious smile. 'Please be seated, Mr Dillard. I'm glad you could come.'

Her features and her voice had that fine-drawnness which is supposed to indicate breeding. She was fashionably attired in an expensive, closely fitting gown of pearl-grey silk that moulded itself to her statuesque figure. As they sat, Joshua had the impression her blue-grey eyes were calmly appraising him and that he met with her approval.

Gossip had it that being a mining

millionaire's maiden sister, Flora Bennett, though a handsome and exciting woman, was a mite forbidding to the average, uncultured Western male. Her gaze could be cold and her tongue sharp with suspicion, they said. Maybe this accounted for her continued spinsterhood at age 28 despite her classical beauty.

Joshua was never a man to be intimidated and was encouraged by the smile. He struggled with the popular notion that Flora Bennett was frigid. He figured she would respond with appropriate warmth to the right person, at the right time and in the right place. Though mere diversion, the line of thought was interesting . . .

He left it to Flora to open the discussion.

'You've probably read the broad details of what happened in the popular scandal sheets,' she said, 'but I'll start at the beginning.'

Joshua nodded. 'If you feel up to it.'

'I do. I was deeply affected by Ryan's murder, but I learned early in life, at the time of my mother's death, that I had to control my emotions and do my weeping in private. Both my parents are now long departed and my attachment to my brother remained strong throughout his career with Mr Allan Pinkerton's detective firm, his subsequent business successes and his marriage to Jennie Kelley.'

Joshua clasped his hands together on the table before him, studied them but said nothing.

'Six months past, my brother's head was blown apart by a blast from a shotgun in the presence of his wife and Joseph Darcy, his private secretary. Mr Darcy was Rye and Jennie's good friend as well as an employee. He was playing the piano accompaniment and Jennie was singing a light air for their mutual entertainment when an intruder broke into the house, burst upon them, and shot Rye dead.'

'All of which was quite unexpected and shocking, of course,' Joshua murmured.

'Well, no,' Flora said bleakly. 'My brother had made enemies during his time with the Pinkertons, as I know you did yourself with equally dire results. Also, it was my brother's favourite piece of advice always to expect the unexpected.'

'So what happened?'

Flora shrugged. 'I'm not at all sure Rye was assassinated by some old enemy. The incontrovertible facts are that he was killed in his own home and that the felon made good his escape. Newspaper speculation drew the inference an armed robbery had gone wrong. The harrowing account has been recorded of how Jennie and Mr Darcy tried to help Rye, although the extent of his injuries suggests to me they would have been instantly fatal.'

'It must have been dreadful for them,' Joshua said.

'I hurried to Denver and was in time for the funeral and the interment at Riverside Cemetery,' Flora went on, hastening to her own experience of the tragedy. 'Rye was well connected, as I'm sure you know. He was a prominent mines investor, merchant and clubman. His friends included Mr Herman Beckurts, editor and owner of the *Denver Tribune*, and Bishop John Spalding, of the Episcopal Church, who were among the cemetery association's original twenty stockholders.'

Joshua silently noted that Flora might be something of a snob, but he would also have to agree that Ryan Bennett had an impressive last resting-place. Riverside was 160 acres of land on the east bank of the South Platte River about four miles downstream from the business district. A credit to the city, it was no Boot Hill and could claim the distinction of being the most beautifully landscaped and appointed cemetery in the Rocky Mountain West.

'The occasion must have been a terrible ordeal for you,' he said, all sympathy.

But she spurned his sombre tone. 'I hated it! The worst part was the smell.

They kept the coffin lid closed, naturally in view of the horrific damage wreaked by the shotgun, but someone, I presume the undertaker, must have drenched my poor brother's body with perfume. That beautiful maplewood coffin reeked of cheap pomade.'

Joshua observed how the unimportant affront seemed to revolve around what she considered tawdry. *Cheap*. Again, the offence she'd taken suggested snobbishness to him. It was time to nudge the conversation toward more significant matters.

'From what you wrote me,' Joshua said, 'I understand you have newer and deeper concerns.'

Her educated voice grew icier.

'Yes, Mr Dillard. I wanted to bring you in because the theories about my brother's death and what has happened since demand further investigation!'

Joshua's eyebrows arched.

'What has happened since . . . ' he said, prompting.

2

Joshua Asks Questions

A flash of annoyance came to Flora Bennett's eyes. One moment she was sitting quite composed, her tilted chin denoting she was calmly resolute and incapable of a covetous thought or lapse from good taste. Then came an abrupt transformation in which her expression became hard and she articulated her real grievance.

'My loss of a brother did not elicit the same public response as the widow's. Mrs Bennett — Jennie — was showered with Denver society's sympathy. I was ignored and the disappearance of a will which I knew gave me a considerable share of Rye's estate was set aside by a lawyer completely under the thumb of Rye's secretary, Joseph Darcy. I'd forgotten my bother's favourite saying.'

'Ah . . . ' Joshua said, thinking he began to understand. 'Always expect the unexpected. A bequest is involved and it was — uh — misplaced.'

'To say the least.'

'There's more?'

'Indeed there is, Mr Dillard. Jennie soon tired of being the centre of popular sentimental attention. She retired from public life. She retained Mr Darcy as her sole spokesman and adviser, sold up the house on Capitol Hill in disgraceful haste, and quit the city. As though she was running away . . . '

'Well, maybe she was,' Joshua said, being reasonable. 'After all, the horrific tragedy — '

Flora scoffed. 'She decamped to Silverville where Rye had held interests in the mines and other property. Do you know Silverville?'

'Passed through it once — typical, small, rough mining settlement.'

'Exactly. I haven't been there myself

— I wouldn't go to such a town under any circumstances — but I am sufficiently well informed to know it would be less than the ideal retreat for a grieving young widow seeking peace and a safe haven from the wilder side of Colorado life.'

'Maybe she has some sort of support there,' Joshua suggested.

'Yes. Mr Joseph Darcy's, rumour has it. He has been using the estate's realized Denver assets for more investment in the town.'

Joshua was shrewd enough to catch the drift of Flora's insinuations. Her brother's widow and his former secretary appeared to have a good thing going in Silverville while she had been cheated of a share of money she thought should have come to her.

Flora hammered home her message.

'The Denver police caught nobody for Rye's murder. The alleged intruder — an armed robber said to have blundered — has gotten clear away. No charges have been laid against anyone.

These are the things that have been allowed to happen and which I want you to put to rights, Mr Dillard.'

The ravings of a jealous, disappointed woman?

Joshua did some quick calculating. He needed a paying assignment, or he'd soon be joining the down-and-outs. He liked Denver. The infant Mile High City was a lively social hub, outwardly prosperous but retaining its character as a Wild West frontier town, albeit with an opera house, high-toned emporiums, mining-machine factories, banks, schools and churches. Yet it took money for a man to foot it in this cosmopolitan beehive. Fact of the matter was, he was running up an embarrassing hotel bill and was having to think twice before he bought a drink, a cigar or even a meal.

Financial hardship, the mother of all hardships, had been a way of life for Joshua since ending his Pinkerton career. He'd survived, but he didn't want to spend the rest of his life getting by on less than nothing.

'Are you suggesting,' Joshua said, carefully determined to get things clear in his mind, 'that Mrs Bennett and Mr Darcy — uh — knew more about your brother's murder than they reported?'

'Yes,' the woman said coolly.

Flora Bennett's unenunciated accusations might have more to do with the imagination of a mean and shallow woman consumed by self-interest than with any conspiracy. But Joshua wasn't quite prepared to refuse his potential client — or to believe her character was that tawdry. She struck him as an intelligent, strong-willed woman who would be capable of recognizing in herself and restraining an unsatisfied appetite for wealth.

Maybe it was that she was just pained by the bitterness of a loved one's loss. He could identify with that.

Joshua pondered. Evidently, from the challenge in her high-held head and steady gaze she expected him to reach a decision now and respond.

Joshua gave a sigh that said he still

had doubts. 'Are you sure you need a man like me, Miss Bennett?'

She favoured him with her most gracious smile. A man might also have had reason to suppose she looked him up and down and liked what she saw. If they hadn't been discussing a business arrangement, her roving gaze could have led Joshua to think she was giving him the eye.

'Quite sure, Mr Dillard. The services of a man of your — shall we say — *bold* reputation are exactly what I require. My brother was sent into oblivion by a blast from a shotgun. It came to me as a shock, because I believed his work no longer brought him in continual contact with the world's scum. I've led a sheltered, quiet life, away from violent people. I've no idea how they have to be dealt with. But I'm very certain that you have wisdom in the world's wickedness, that you'll have no compunctions about using your skills as necessary. I can pay the expenses. I can also give a written guarantee that when the matter is brought to a successful outcome — and I'm in possession of what rightfully should be mine — a percentage of the reward will be yours.'

Joshua was a little startled. 'Is that all?' he asked, intending the question as an ironical comment on the generosity of the arrangement.

But Flora was in no frame of mind to recognize humour applied to her most serious ambition. A steeliness came to her eye and she responded by making an additional proposal.

She turned from his face and gazed, probably unseeingly, toward the window and its view of the ebb and flow of the urban street and the aloofness of the distant mountains.

She said resolutely, 'No, perhaps that isn't enough, given the uncertainty of the outcome and that you might be endangering your own life in pursuit of my brother's killer.'

She turned back to him, moistened her upper lip with a flick of her tongue and revealed in a rush just how much she had checked out his background.

'Mr Dillard, I understand that like many other gentlemen who visit Denver City you occasionally frequent the houses on The Row. Indeed, I'm sure you have better justification than those with wives or sweethearts in their lives, and yours is a lonely life . . . '

Joshua thought what the hell is she driving at? Though he was beginning to guess, he said nothing.

Flora's cheeks took on a modicum of colour. 'As you know,' she went on, 'I was acquainted with your late wife — a most wholesome and charming young woman who, like my brother, is no longer with us. That leaves you and I with something in common — we are both without emotional attachment or responsibility in a world that seldom offers us personal comforts. I therefore can promise that as soon as the truth emerges about Rye's death — when you bring me the necessary information to support charges — I will be ready to entertain you more warmly than would the cold fish that Denver society paints me.'

Joshua was momentarily rocked. It was a pretty little speech, carefully worded, and it would be tasteless to ask a determined lady who was more than the Holladay Street wenches, to whom she'd alluded, to dot the i's and cross the t's.

Take on the job of finding and exposing whoever had killed Ryan Bennett and Flora Bennett would express her gratitude in coin that predated history.

Joshua was flattered by this Queen of Sheba's faith in his abilities. It sounded like she thought he had the wisdom of a Solomon where frontier crime was involved. How did it go?

'And she gave the king an hundred and twenty talents of gold ... And king Solomon gave unto the queen of Sheba all her desire, whatsoever she asked ... '

But it wasn't such promised benefi-cence that finally swayed Joshua. His decision to take up the affair came down to the bedrock of the original considerations that he was near flat-broke; that Flora's brother, like himself, had served with and quit the Pinkertons; that Flora was someone who'd known his lost wife.

Thus, though wondering if he was a double-dyed fool, the thing was done. He hired on as Flora Bennett's private detective and started out on the impractical business of solving a case the Denver papers said the police had given up on, baffled.

The trail of Bennett's killer was grown very cold.

In the days that followed, Joshua probed the mystery of the man who'd come from nowhere, done his dastardly deed and disappeared. Having a mind and methods of his own, Joshua wasn't prepared to discount the person's very existence on the say-so of Flora Bennett. He didn't tell her — because she was a client he didn't want to lose — but he regarded her as prejudiced and his mission next to impractical.

He roamed the city asking questions, particularly of the people who walked its streets after dark. Did they remember seeing a stranger on the night Ryan Bennett, prominent businessman, mines investor and clubman, was murdered in his home by a prowler with a shotgun? Had they seen the man since? Where was he now? Who was he?

He gravitated to Denver's shadier quarters — the places a visiting desperado might be expected to sit and rest if only for the briefest spell during a visit designed to carry out a robbery or make a revenge killing.

A loquacious drinker in a stuffy saloon a block away from Larimer Street, where the city's high rollers spent freely in the gaming houses, put him on a particular track. He leaned on the bar alongside of Joshua, admired the glass he, Joshua, had paid for the apron to fill, and said owlishly, 'If you were a wandering man and had come to this here fair metropolis from afar — as any stranger is obliged to do on account of its location six hundred mile from the nearest like! — what would you spare time for, aside or ahead of pressing business?'

'A beer or two with a friendly citizen?' Joshua hazarded hopefully.

The half-drunk thumped the bar with his fist.

'Nope! I reckon it'd be a woman. Ain't the word put out across the West that we have here a special kind of paradise? The swankiest parlour houses? The highest-toned bordellos? Talk to the girls in those, friend. There you'll cut sign, if there be any.'

'Could be punishing on the pocket-book . . . ' Joshua mused.

His adviser chuckled. 'But contrari-wise, no chore!'

Joshua shrugged. 'Ah well, a man will do what he must.'

The job could be a lengthy undertaking. But the notion held promise. It was a line of inquiry not likely to have been pursued by strait-laced, official lawmen.

Denver had a sporting life at all levels, from the august to the squalid. The red-light district boasted upmarket palaces where no expense had been spared on lavish if sometimes garish decor; at the opposite end of the scale, it had places that were small, two-room cribs. Additionally, many saloon girls and hostesses did extra work above bars and back of dance halls, with less protection but without any of the earnings having to be set aside to pay the licence fees that boosted municipal revenues, as was the case with their sisters in the parlour houses.

Joshua made inquiries in Holladay Street. An early break was given him at one of the expensive establishments by a helpful madam. She pragmatically accepted he had his mind on something less profitable to her than dalliance under a mirrored ceiling. After listening to his questions, she directed him to Hattie Soames's place, a mid-range parlour house she said catered especially for the out-of-town transient.

Hattie, a big and busty woman, told him, 'I know nothing about any stranger with a shotgun who visited on the night you mention. In this line, it can be dangerous to discuss a client's business, but I believe I've got a young lady who entertained such a man. She might talk . . . '

She added forthrightly, shrewdly, 'Time has to be paid for, of course. Five dollars an hour, twenty for all night. Miss Virtue is a very popular girl.'

Well, with a name like that — was it really her legal moniker? — she just had to be, Joshua thought.

He handed over five dollars of his precious expenses money.

Virtue came clothed in a very short, low-cut, spangled dress, black silk stockings and high-heeled shoes. She took him by the hand and led him to an upstairs room redolent of rotgut liquor, stale sweat and cheap perfume.

There was no dignity in Virtue's costume, but when she smiled a painted smile and promptly proceeded to peel it off, Joshua demurred.

'I don't give a damn for that stuff,' he lied. 'Leave it lay. What I want to do is talk.'

3

Dove's Tales

'Takes all kinds, I guess,' Virtue said. Her voice was tinged with hurt, or maybe it was disappointment. 'Howsoever, Hattie Soames don't give no refunds.'

Joshua said, 'I won't be claiming any. All I want to know is what you remember of a man who came here carrying a shotgun the night Ryan Bennett was murdered. You hear about the killing?'

The girl looked guilty.

'Yeah. Who didn't? But it ain't nothin' concernin' me. A workin' girl has to be careful what she says. It's private, ain't it? Conqui — consi — confi — '

'Confidential,' Joshua supplied for her. 'What do you know about that man with his shotgun? You could have got yourself shot back there. Didn't you think it odd?'

'I suppose . . . '

'You don't sound like you were worried.'

She got huffy. 'Why should I been? I please men, don't I? Whatever he wanted to do to me, he wouldn't've been hankerin' to shoot me!'

'What can you tell me about him?'

'He was real fast . . . like a fumblin' kid or a feller who'd gone without in a coon's age. But most of all he smelled somethin' fierce. I'll always remember the smell. Bad as skunk.'

Abruptly, Joshua tossed at her, 'What was his name?'

'Zach — S-Skann.'

She broke hesitantly after the first name, like she was wishing she'd thought about it before starting to answer. She swallowed fearfully.

'I don't know nothin' else about him, I swear. I only seen him the once. I don't want no trouble.'

'Zach Skann . . . ' The name sounded vaguely familiar to Joshua.

'You want to take your pleasure, mister, or don't you?'

Virtue's voice wobbled and Joshua figured that between her apprehension and her previous firmness about her ignorance, he was going to learn no more.

But he was suspicious and he made one last try.

'You make a habit of learning and memorizing casual clients' names?'

' 'Course not! I guess he must've told me after he found out mine.'

Joshua shook his head wonderingly, still pondering on where he'd come across the name Zach Skann before. Moreover, was Virtue telling the truth about how she'd learned it?

Then the girl flung her arms around him and pulled him close to her with simulated passion. She was warm and scented and eager to please.

'You ain't just passing through are you, mister? You'll be stopping a whiles.'

She made her interest sound excitingly personal. 'Coming plenty . . . '

Joshua grated, 'I don't want you, Virtue.' And he disengaged from her with clammy hands.

★ ★ ★

Immediately after Joshua Dillard left, the girl called Virtue pulled on a hooded cloak, hiding her supposed finery, and slipped downstairs.

'Where do you think you're going?' Hattie Soames said.

'To see a man.'

'You see men here, dearie.'

'I didn't mean like that. There's something I think this gent'll pay me cash money to hear. I know where to find him — Reilly's Exchange on Twentieth Street. I'll be back directly.'

She scooted out the door before buxom Hattie could raise any protest, let alone rise and stop her.

'You be careful at Reilly's, gal,' Hattie rumbled ominously but only to herself.

'Those as think they're smart is apt to end up floating face down in Cherry Creek!'

Denver had been termed 'the great braggart city' and Reilly's Exchange enjoyed an unsavoury reputation as one of its most rugged watering holes. Loners came off the mountains and the plains to spend the savings of months of hard work in the wildest dissipation. Reilly's was a stamping-ground of choice where the outcast might embark on a spree and the barkeeps knew it was wise to turn a blind eye to the shenanigans. Seldom a night passed when a brawl didn't erupt. Men were shot, cut, killed. Hunters, trappers, teamsters and Ute Indians found in Reilly's an escape valve for the steam of their frustrations.

On the thin borderline of lawlessness, it was not a safe place for an unaccompanied and attractive female.

Virtue pulled up her hood, huddled into her cloak and was pleased to see Cord Skann in open view, leaning idly against the long bar. It was still early and few frontier loafers were present of the type disinclined to respect the restraints of civilization.

Cord Skann was a big, raw-boned man with strongly defined features: a large nose, long, straggly black hair, thick, bushy black eyebrows. Unshaven for a while, which made him look unkempt and a little dirty. She hurried over and leaned on the bar alongside him, keeping her back to the room.

'Cord,' she said breathlessly. 'A gent came to see me. He was asking questions about that man you told me was your brother, Zach.'

Skann thought about it a moment, the heavy brows lowering.

'Is that so? Well, what in hell . . . ? Did you tell him anythin'?'

'What could I? Only the little I told you. That your brother came to see me just the once, on the night Ryan Bennett was killed. That he stayed only briefly and hasn't shown again since. He's on the dodge, ain't he?'

Skann scowled. 'Ain't for me or you to say. Tell me this sticky beak's name.'

'I didn't ask.'

Skann grinned unpleasantly, unmoved by the professional pout of her full, ripe lips.

'Then if you know what's good for you, gal, you're gonna have to enquire, ain't you? Somethin's wrong here . . . almighty wrong. I came to Denver to find out what. Get me the gent's name! The boys an' I will make it our business to l'arn what he knows that we don't . . . '

Virtue was disappointed. Instead of easy money, she'd been given work to do and a veiled threat had been made. She'd hoped to be shut of the affair with a quick reward.

Skann looked her over, scowling. 'If'n I was you, I'd just cut along an' get that name real fast. Else next time I come callin' at Hattie's, I won't be easy on you!'

Though she was shocked to the fullest extent she ever was by what men did or said, she went without protest. A girl had to do what she was told when a man cut up rough. The punishment promised if she didn't would be harder and dirtier than the job he'd given her.

The note of menace in Skann's voice put a shiver down her spine and lent wings to her feet. Working girls were totally vulnerable. Only a damn fool of a dove didn't learn quick how to judge when an unstable gent's temper was about to explode.

★ ★ ★

Joshua Dillard left Hattie Soames's house with reason for satisfaction. He had made a beginning. He had a name. Zach Skann. What he had to do now was find out something about Skann. To discover who he was and decide whether his visit to Denver had been connected with the Bennett case . . . to locate his present whereabouts.

What excited Joshua further, once he'd made good his escape from the distraction of Virtue's company, was a strong conviction that Zach Skann was a name he'd come across previously, maybe during his time with the Pinkerton Detective Agency. It was more than slightly possible the name had also been linked in some way with that of the brother agent he'd never met, Ryan Bennett.

He'd been trained to have a good memory for names, but no one could carry everything in their head for year after year of the kind of life he led. Fortunately, he still had connections with the agency and one of them was his old supervisor in Chicago, Boise 'Boss' Flagler, who was directly answerable to 'Mr William', elder son of founder Allan Pinkerton.

Mr William was a stickler for record-keeping and believed anything about anyone could be contained in a file, complete with pictures. The mugshot was a Pinkerton innovation. The agency already boasted it had the biggest collection of outlaws' pictures in the world. As criminals and crimes made the newspapers, field agents diligently clipped and sent in every story with their own added comments. The material went into each crook's growing file. It was this library that was partly responsible for the growing Pinkerton legend.

Joshua knew that through the good offices of Boss Flagler he still had access to these vital records. He went briskly uptown to the telegraph office and drafted a wire to be sent to Flagler, Pinkerton national headquarters, Chicago.

'Is that Pinkerton's the detective agency?' the operator asked in hushed tones. 'Them as never goes to bed?'

'Sure is,' Joshua said. The clerk plainly had in mind the symbol of the large staring eye with the slogan 'We never sleep' that was emblazoned on the agency's building.

Joshua confidently left the dutiful operator to tap away at his instrument, giving instructions for any reply to be brought to him instantly at his hotel. He imagined Flagler in his faraway office, scratching the bushy fringe of beard on his otherwise clean-shaven face and muttering, 'Now what the devil is Dillard on to here?'

After his visit with Virtue, Joshua felt ready for a lie-down — could he be getting old? — and he paused only to shrug off his coat and kick off his boots before flopping on to his room's narrow bed.

From outside came the sounds of the street: the creak of wagons and carriages, the clop of hoofs, the sporadic buzz of greetings and other, indiscernible exchanges between passing pedestrians. Inside, a green-bodied blowfly droned around lazily in the heat and occasionally pinged against window glass.

Joshua stared up at the smoke-browned, flaking paint of the ceiling. He tried to recap on what he'd learned from Virtue. Depending on what Flagler turned up for him, it could be everything or nothing.

He wondered if there was a picture of a Zach Skann; if it could be sent up from Chicago; how many days that would take; if Virtue could be prevailed upon to confirm the identity of her visitor and Ryan Bennett's likely killer . . .

Diverted into thinking about the unaptly named young woman, he drowsed.

Later — he didn't know how much later — a knock came at his door. Joshua came instantly alert like an awakened creature of the wild. A boy delivered into his hands an envelope from the telegraph office.

He ripped it open and unfolded the flimsy sheets inside. The message, though sparsely written, gave Joshua everything he had hoped for. Once jogged, his memory was able to fill several of the gaps to be expected in a telegram.

That Skann, of course . . .

He determined immediately that he

should make a report in person to Flora Bennett.

She was going to be pleased with this information, very pleased, he thought. He had a prime suspect, a motive and could probably — in due course, with Virtue's assistance — prove presence and opportunity.

Obviously he still had to find Zach Skann. That was going to be the hardest part of his assignment. Perhaps he would have to enlist outside help — the Pinks were a distinct possibility, which could prove a financial bother. However, in consideration of their prior involvement, chances were good they might be willing to pitch in without extra charge to Miss Bennett or a diminution of his own fee by splitting.

In an optimistic frame of mind, he sent a note to Flora Bennett, saying he was in receipt of significant information and asking if he could see her at the earliest convenience.

She replied that she would like that and it was arranged for them to get together at the same hotel — far grander than Joshua's dingy lodging — where they'd earlier conferred and she'd hired him to enquire into her brother's gruesome death.

This time, they met in Flora Bennett's accommodation at the hotel, a luxurious private suite. Joshua was looking forward to receiving Flora's interest and gratitude, in savouring the fruit of a prompt if not yet complete victory.

But when he presented his evidence, such as it was, the atmosphere took on an acute frostiness.

Flora Bennett was far from pleased.

4

Facts...? Fiddlesticks!

They sat in a bay window with a breathtaking view of the mountains. The top sash was open and the room was light and airy and cool. Flora Bennett wore a flowing, champagne-coloured gown with a generously cut neckline below strands of pearls. She looked wonderful and had welcomed him smiling dazzlingly. But now she looked icy, just as Joshua felt his temperature rising.

'It's mere theory, Mr Dillard,' she said coldly, 'and no better than a sister's intuition, which suggests other explanations.'

Joshua shrugged his shoulders and strived to keep calm. He had to make allowances. She'd missed out on a heap of dinero as well as lost a brother; she was desperate to continue living a sweet life to which she was accustomed; lastly, you never argued with the person who was hiring you.

He said with a great show of patience, 'I'm sorry but the information I have does fit.'

'Hmm! I'd be sorry, too.'

He explained again. 'Your brother's assassination purely looks a vengeance killing. Zach Skann was a leader of a secret society of coal miners in Pennsylvania fifteen years back. Such societies were fighting for better labour conditions, using threats, beatings, riots and murder against abusive mine owners, supervisors, police . . . anyone who worked against them.'

'Like Ryan,' Flora said bitterly.

'I fear so. After the Civil War, Pinkerton agents played major roles in several clashes between workers and management. Allan Pinkerton's early method of infiltrating criminal groups has since been imitated and perfected by federal and metropolitan forces, yet its success ultimately lay with the skill of the operative. Your brother was good at the work, especially where it involved the business world and mining.'

Flora listened in sulky silence.

Joshua pressed on levelly, trying to inject a note of reasonableness into his voice.

'Rye Bennett infiltrated Skann's society and his spying for the mine managers was instrumental in securing for Skann a long stretch in the penitentiary. Other members of the society were hanged. At his sentencing, Zach Skann raved against Rye, vowing vengeance. Skann was released from the pen at the end of his term just weeks before Rye's murder. These are all facts, recorded by the Pinkertons.'

'Facts . . . ? Fiddlesticks!' Flora said coldly. 'It clears up nothing. Where is this obvious suspect now? And how has he been able to escape the attention of the law?'

Joshua spread his hands in resignation. 'I don't know, but I think we now have a name for your brother's assassin. A full description, maybe a portrait picture, can be mailed out all over from Chicago. I agree, the case is incomplete — '

'I certainly think so, Mr Dillard! For a detective, you have a surprisingly . . . uncomplicated mind.'

Joshua had the notion she'd been about to say 'a simple mind' but had thought better of it.

'How so?'

Flora's snort was ladylike only by a miracle.

'Need I remind you that the Denver newspapers were persuaded my brother's death occurred during a botched armed robbery of his house? Indeed, it may have been fixed to *look* like that afterwards. But why and by whom if, as you submit, it was a revenge killing? I agree Rye could have been shotgunned by an old enemy, but it seems distinctly possible to me that if this was the case, the villain was assisted.'

Joshua had heard her insinuations

before, but he couldn't help a startled query.

'Assisted?'

'How else did a man fresh from a penitentiary contrive to disappear so completely? Why is it the only witness who saw a figure with a shotgun fleeing Capitol Hill insisted the time of the sighting was a quarter-hour or more after the fatal shooting, after it had begun raining?'

'These lines of inquiry have already been pursued by the official law,' Joshua said. 'What would you have me do?'

'I think you should go to Silverville and confront Mrs Bennett and Mr Darcy face to face with your findings. I'd like their reaction closely observed when they're made aware you're investigating the movements of a bad man called Zach Skann.'

So there it was, on the table, Joshua acknowledged silently. Flora predicated everything on the supposition that her sister-in-law and the secretary knew more than they had revealed; that they were somehow involved in her brother's murder and had cheated her of a small fortune.

To say she was hostile toward Jennie Bennett and Joseph Darcy was putting it mildly. She might not have declared it, but she was convinced at the very least they had put over a clever swindle with regard to her brother's will.

It sounded from what she'd told Joshua before that they were prospering and had entered into a rather close, bordering scandalous, relationship in a wild mining town. But did this suggest they were guilty of complicity in Ryan Bennett's murder? That they knew of Zach Skann and would put him on Skann's trail?

The suggested course of challenging interrogation struck Joshua as high-handed.

'Have you considered accompanying me?' he asked tentatively, thinking, some hope!

'Of course not, Mr Dillard! I'm not cut out for that. I prefer civilized towns and cities. I would like to go back East. Maybe to Europe. But on my present limited finances that's impossible. I don't like much of the West. Only Denver has come close to offering a style of life into which I could fit pleasantly. Is that completely selfish?'

Joshua didn't try to reply to the question, not wanting to allow the conversation to veer off at an unproductive tangent.

His opinion was that Silverville would be a wild-goose chase, but he could scarcely afford to abandon his commission now. And Flora's supreme air of certainty defied anyone to give her back-talk.

He sighed. 'I'll need more expenses money to get me to Silverville . . . '

'You have it, Mr Dillard.'

'These mining towns are tolerable pricey, rootin'-tootin' places, given over some to extortion. I'll need eating money, too. Will the allowance cover it?'

'It's covered.'

Joshua invested most of the money in a dun mare that reminded him in temperament of an easy-going chestnut he'd once ridden called Polly.

The mare's nondescript colour masked an alert willingness Joshua liked in a saddle horse. He wasn't fond of having to claw leather on a crow hopper or a cloud hunter. In his line of work, an obedient, equable horse could be the difference between life and death in a moment of crisis. It made sense to avoid a salty bronc you could be damn sure would kick the lid off when men started burning powder, for example.

Kiss the ground in those circumstances and you were headed for the misty beyond, pronto.

The dun confirmed his judgement, being clear-footed on the rutted, hard-used road that stretched west from Denver to Silverville. A good, fit horse could cover the fortysome miles in a day. It didn't sound a lot, but

Joshua knew it would call for a mite of trotting and cantering to achieve an overall pace of about five miles an hour.

As the sun moved over and ahead of him into the western sky, the trail took more and more twists and turns, through shadowed canyons with near-perpendicular sides and along shelves with precipitous drop-offs into nothingness on one side.

In places close to the road, the more accessible slopes had been denuded of timber, carried away as lumber for Colorado's ubiquitous mining operations. The plundering of greenery had left scars that brought a stony bleakness to the scenery. But yonder, the Rockies' grandeur was restored by the unravageable peaks above the timberline. They were iced with brilliant white snow that hadn't melted despite the intense sunlight.

The dun lived up to Joshua's expectations and nervy moments were few despite the going verging on difficult. His horse's confident performance and the dry air encouraged serious, clear-headed thinking about his mission.

It wasn't difficult to figure how Flora Bennett wanted his imagination to run. Flora was hungry for money — a portion of her brother's fortune. He was meant to suppose Mrs Jennie Bennett and the secretary Joseph Darcy had arranged a jackleg lawyer to mislay Ryan Bennett's will, then as quickly as possible had turned whatever they could into cash and negotiable securities and decamped to Silverville to start over beyond the survey of Denver city's scandalized eyes.

But neither he nor Flora had evidence to prove a thing. Not one damned thing. He could sniff around in Silverville, but he hadn't worked out yet how he could barge in on the pair of lovebirds — if that was what they were — and presumptuously accuse them of being conspirators in the murder of the woman's husband.

He wondered if Jennie Bennett had taken up with her husband's secretary only since Ryan Bennett's death — or was it a liaison that had been in secret progress for much longer than that?

While he was mulling on how he might answer this question in Silverville when he might do better to probe in Denver, the first hint of lurking trouble made itself evident.

The dun's ears pricked up and flicked forward. Simultaneously, he felt uneasy himself. The horse didn't become skittish, but it was on edge.

He was riding through the deep hollow of a canyon. Down here the sun had already set and it lay in cold shadow — a spooky twilight that didn't strike man or animal as natural for the time of day.

The roadway had been widened in places for coaches and wagons by blasting. The rubble had been carted on to other spots where it had been tipped into the bed of the river that ran through the canyon. Thus it served a double purpose for the dynamiting, since the partial filling-in of the river formed a foundation for more widening of the broadly parallel trail.

The work was rough and poorly finished. Footing in all places was uneven. Larger rocks and explosive-shattered boulders had been left where they'd tumbled. They stuck up like giants' rotten teeth, grey and weather-stained where they hadn't been split asunder.

Joshua followed the dun's searching look across the ravished terrain. The jumble of bald rocks provided places of concealment. Elsewhere, ahead, a few stunted pines and cedars, spared by the miners because of their inaccessibility, offered more.

The feeling grew in him. There was something, someone out there, waiting. His mouth had gone dry and his stomach felt the strange emptiness of premonition.

An ambush? Road agents? A holdup?

Joshua wasn't carrying any riches. Nor did he look a well-heeled traveller. His garb was worn and made to look shabbier by trail dust that clung to it like grey gunpowder. The dust's grittiness was also apparent to him in the creases of his face as he narrowed his eyes.

But such wealth as he had — his allowance from Flora Bennett — he couldn't afford to lose. He had no intention of arriving in Silverville with nothing but one thin dime, if he was lucky.

Off to his left, a short distance back, he'd passed a steep gash cut in the canyon's side by a mountain torrent fed by snow melt from higher regions and debouching in a cloud of spray into the slower-running river.

The dun whickered. Joshua thought he saw movement uptrail in the shadows of the rock maze.

It was enough for a solitary rider to decide on defensive action. With a tug, he wheeled the dun and headed back the way he'd come, kicking with his heels and lashing with the rein ends. The obedient horse knew what was wanted and broke into a gallop.

From behind, he heard angry cries, ordering him to halt. Glancing back he saw two riders in pursuit. One had a Winchester rifle which he flung to his shoulder and fired.

Accurate shooting from horseback at a man also on horseback and at a distance of more than three hundred yards was no easy feat. Joshua trusted to luck and kept going.

Reaching the tributary mountain stream where it joined the river, he pulled the horse into its steep course. Fetlock deep, the dun started climbing gamely.

They never reached the possible safety of higher, wilder country.

From the road below, the man with the Winchester fired again. This time he'd figured his chances of stopping Joshua's flight would be better if he aimed at something bigger than a man-sized target.

He aimed for the horse. Even so, he missed and it was only a trick of fate that caused the bullet to ricochet off a rock and tear cruelly into the animal's belly as the jagged piece of hot metal it had become.

Crazy-blind with pain, the splashing dun no longer responded to Joshua's direction. It lunged up out of the shallow, fast-flowing stream, leaving it pink with swirls of blood. Joshua cussed as he lost control. The dun was a good horse and had done harm to no one.

Its rider forgotten, the dun charged glancingly into the trunk of a stunted but sturdy pine that had withstood the buffeting of the elements and could take this latest assault, too.

Joshua's right foot was knocked clean out of the stirrup. Bruised or broken, his leg was kicking free, nerveless, so he found himself rolling to his left side, with no means to stop the roll. The reins were jerked from his hands. He snatched for them, missed, found instead a risky grip on the pommel, which was covered with leather, shiny and smooth from use.

Unable to check the frenzied horse, clinging on to the saddle but liable to slip any moment, Joshua feared he might eventually be dragged or that the horse would fall, roll and trap him by the leg or more. So he let his left foot out of the stirrup, too.

Immediately his boot left the stirrup, he went headlong out, sideways and down. It might indeed have proved the best course he could have taken but for the terrain. It was rough and the horse was moving too fast and too erratically for him to make fine calculations.

He crashed into a small, lichen-splotched boulder. He hit it head on.

Pain exploded inside his skull.

Maybe after making another fifty yards, the wounded dun had stumbled again and was collapsing, making a horrible, retching, squealing sound he'd never heard the like of from human or critter.

He hoped his unknown attackers would have the mercy to put it out of its misery quickly.

It was the last thought he had before a great roaring filled his cracked head like a deafening waterfall and the black pit of unconsciousness opened for him and swallowed him up.

5

An Ally Called Poverty Joe

First to register was the sound of men's voices, echoing as though through a long dark tunnel. Consciousness was pain. His limbs twitched, yet were heavy as lead. He heard somebody groan quietly, very close by, before he realized it was himself. But there were also the men's words. He struggled with reluctance back to a wakefulness which instinct told him was best kept hidden.

His head beat with trip-hammer blows as he tried to make sense of what the men were saying.

'Idiots, you could've killed the tricky bastard. I said I didn't want no shootin'. Dead men tell nothin'.'

'He would've gotten away contrari-wise, Cord.'

'Naw, Virg, it's plain as the nose on

your face. The ex-Pink was headed for Silverville an' we would've gotten another chance when he took up the trail again. Powerful determined bastards, Pinks. It's Silverville where Rye Bennett's widow has set up. Mebbe this clever dick figures she knows more than she's let on. An' if that's so, mebbe it's like we been guessin' — she also knows what happened to Zach after he blasted her stinkin' man to hell.'

Joshua heard a clink of metal on metal on metal, the slosh of poured liquid, and the harsh aroma of strong coffee wafted to him.

'We sure as hell don't,' another man grumbled. 'Zach might've vanished off the face of the earth. Ditched us, anyways.'

The man called Cord swallowed noisily and said with some force, 'My brother ain't like that, Slim. There has to be a reason.'

Except for the men's talk and small movements, the place he was in was as silent and cold as an empty church.

Joshua drew three swift conclusions from the testy exchange. The man in charge was called Cord. He was a brother of Zach Skann, the missing alleged assassin of Ryan Bennett. He didn't want him, Joshua Dillard, dead.

He decided it might be safe to discontinue playing possum. He made a move to sit up but his surroundings, once glimpsed, began to whirl, so he lay back again. Blood throbbed through his head.

'Where am I?' he asked. Prosaic, non-confrontational.

'See? He ain't hurt too bad,' Virg said. 'Jest a heavy knock on the noggin.'

'Long as it ain't busted his mem'ry,' Cord said.

Joshua willed his eyes to focus.

He was on an uneven floor in a dark, candlelit passage. The roof overhead and the walls to each side were rock, spanned and shored by heavy timbers. He had to be underground.

'Where am I?' he repeated.

'The Maybelline No. 1. Abandoned

mine. Closed up. Good for a private camp.'

His informant was Virg, a medium-built fellow of about twenty-five with hair the colour of dirty hay and squinty eyes.

Cord said drily, 'The idea was he'd be answerin' the questions.'

Cord Skann was tall and broad-shouldered. Big nose. Black hair, bushy eyebrows, no intended moustache but in need of a shave and with stubbled jowls. The face was stony, humourless. His eyes were bright and hard as chips of obsidian. His jaw jutted aggressively. He looked a mean man to mess with.

But Joshua was not one to be intimidated by looks.

'Who are you? What do you want?'

'Full of 'em, ain't he?' Slim said.

'Crazy,' Virg said.

Cord stated, 'You're an ex-Pink name of Joshua Dillard and you been askin' questions 'bout my brother, Zach Skann. A whore in Denver told me this, so it ain't no use denyin' it if'n that's how your mind's workin'.'

Joshua's head was pounding.

'My mind isn't working; it's hurting. Your pal here shot my horse which dumped me headfirst on rocks. I think I'm owed a right to ask questions.'

Skann's black, hairy nostrils flared. He snorted mirthlessly.

'So am I! My brother does the world a favour executing a high-an'-mighty bastard. Then he disappears offa the face of the earth an' another god-damned ex-Pink starts poking into the affair. I wanna know what the hell is going on!'

Joshua took a line of reason. 'Questions do get asked about men who set themselves up to play executioner, common though it might be in places where's there's little law.'

The calm reply produced another snort.

'My brother followed his conscience. A morally minded man, Zach. Well, hear this, Dillard — I figure my brother's a blinkered fool. I ain't never had none of his social-justice pretensions. I don't play the world's rotten game. They call me an outlaw, pure an' simple, an' I guess I am. I help myself to what I want. Presently, this happens to be finding out where my brother is.'

His face tightened with snarl of bitterness. 'I suspicion he's run foul of some dirty deal. When I know what it is, I'll do what's apt.'

His vehemence added to Joshua's unease. He recognized in Cord Skann a dangerous, frightening man. Cautiously, he asked, 'For why did Rye Bennett deserve to die? He did what was expected of him by the Pinkerton Agency, but he bailed out of that organization some years back, same as me. He made a new life, became a respectable, self-made businessman.'

Skann was not to be appeased. Nor would he let Joshua turn the tables and become the interrogator.

'Sure, Bennett went to church regular, worshipped his Creator,' he said bleakly. 'Like all the self-made men do. 'Sides, it would've taken more'n his

69

money to wash off the blood that was on his hands. You're hired by his sister, ain't you? She ain't no friend of the widow. What's she told you?'

'Certainly nothing about your brother. Like you, she doesn't reckon things are above board in respect of the Widow Bennett and the secretary, Joseph Darcy. She wants me to go to Silverville and ask questions.'

Skann, consumed by his own wild imaginings, was unconvinced. He appealed to his sidekicks.

'Jesus, the great detective can tell us nothin' we don't know! How do you take that? Do we think he's tellin' the truth?'

Slim said, 'Nope. All Pinks lie.' He was a thin, narrow-faced man who looked and sounded perpetually caustic.

'Feller, it's God's truth,' Joshua said. 'Could be Zach is being real careful, hiding out. He may've crossed a border, north or south. Wanted men do.'

Skann said, 'We don't believe he'd

leave us in the dark. He'd send word. We're talkin' 'bout his kin, his friends. We reckon you must be on to somethin'.'

Joshua shrugged, but kept his lips buttoned.

The appropriate 'Suit yourself' would be inflammatory. Whatever he said, he wouldn't be able to satisfy this bunch. He'd already suffered at their hands and there was a cruelty, a fanaticism, about Cord Skann that suggested any interest he had in his well-being would evaporate if he could indeed convince him he was ignorant of the present fortunes of brother Zach who'd avenged his hanged coal-miner comrades with a scattergun.

He'd heard Cord say it, more or less: a dead man would tell nothing. That was why he'd had to be taken alive. It was fair to assume it was why for now he would be kept alive.

Joshua's head ached, he felt nauseous and, were he given the chance, he wasn't sure he could so much as stand.

His legs might buckle under him like rubber.

Cord was full of angry doubt. It was patent in the man's rigid, taut stance. But it was Cord who in fact forced himself to use the very words that had been on Joshua's lips.

'Suit yourself, mister,' he snarled, standing over him. 'You won't hold out on us long, damn you. We're goin' back up top to our cosy quarters in the old mine buildings. We'll leave you roped up here for the night, in the pitch black with just the rats for company. Mebbe you'll be a mite more willin' to tell tomorrow. If that don't work, Slim knows a few Comanche tricks that loosen tongues real good.'

Joshua stayed silent.

Slim studied him like a butcher eyeing a carcass.

'He won't aim to fool with you none,' Cord said. 'I'm glad I ain't you.'

Virg said, 'I don't like the air down here. Let's go brew ourselves another pot of coffee an' be comf'table.' He produced a malicious grin.

Thus it was that both sides played stubbornly for time. They didn't know that while the game was afoot the initiative would be snatched from them.

★   ★   ★

It was a crawling time of pain and thirst for Joshua that he had no means to measure. Albeit his head continued to swim in the blackness and at times he lapsed into blessed unawareness, he guessed many hours had passed before a glimmer of distant light impinged on his consciousness.

Shortly, shuffling and swearing followed. It wasn't the scuttle or squeak of the promised infesting rats.

'Over here,' he croaked, not knowing to whom he was betraying his presence, whether it would be friend or enemy.

'Damn me . . . I spied it right,' the unknown said. 'They left him down here and he isn't a dead 'un yet.'

The light was a bobbing bull's-eye

lantern. It drew near, momentarily became a dazzle and was placed on the floor. A face, partly illuminated, loomed over Joshua.

It looked an old face, but the flickering lantern, even with the metal slide fully open, carved deep shadows. Moreover, the face was bearded and had bristly side whiskers that extended well over the cheekbones. With the tufted eyebrows they made something close to a mask. Age uncertain, Joshua corrected his initial impression. A grizzly porcupine but maybe not so old.

'Trussed up and not in good shape, are you, sir?' his finder opined. 'Not gents you want to run foul of, the Skann bunch, but I can cut you free and guide you out. It'll be a pleasure, in point of fact, though I should warn I'm a dangerous man to offend!'

The voice was an educated man's. Its possessor's dress was the near rags of an old hobo, though the worn coat was serviceable, having a sheepskin lining and big collar.

Joshua's head filled with questions, but the blood thundered in his ears with every word he tried to speak, every limited move he tried to make.

'Be obliged,' he managed.

'Are you going to be all right?' his self-appointed rescuer asked. The enquiry dissolved into drumming echoes, then a deafening, sickening buzz.

'I think it's concussion,' Joshua said, his own voice sounding far away. 'I've been hit on the head before, but nothing like this.'

And though he willed himself to be lucid, to feel better, it didn't work. The moment he was cut free from his bonds, and tried to get to his feet, the floor tilted up sharply, he staggered and his world spiralled down into another roaring blackness.

His helper must have been fit, probably strong. His next recollection was that he'd been dragged or supported to a wooden elevator platform, about four feet square, and they were using it to make a shaking, rattling ascent of a shaft.

The man in hobo garb winched them up slowly and jerkily by means of a hand-operated windlass that wound cable on to a drum. It was a makeshift modification of an arrangement that in the Maybelline's productive time had probably been powered by a steam donkey engine. At the top, the crude elevator was made fast with ropes provided for the purpose.

They were in a tumbledown shed that only partly covered the shaft entrance and was filled with the rusting iron framework of machinery that hadn't been worth removing. The cool night air sparked another spell of lucidity for Joshua, though his knees showed an alarming tendency to fold up beneath him. He hoped this was a temporary result of being tightly bound, of cramp or interrupted circulation, rather than of his head injury.

'Thank you,' he said after being helped off the elevator platform. 'My name's Dillard, Joshua Dillard. And I'm indebted to . . . ?'

'They call me Poverty Joe in Silverville, but there's more they don't know than they know. Hah!'

Cryptic, Joshua thought.

They left the shed and picked their way down a steep slope stripped of timber long past. The rotting stumps of pines had been left as obstacles to trip an unwary foot in the dark, along with loose rocks and slips of dust and tailings. In wise consideration of Joshua's condition, they took the descent slowly.

A mountain stream tumbled noisily through the lot, channelled past a big, high shed where an old waterwheel was fixed to the outer wall. In the mine's heyday, the stream plainly had been utilized to drive machinery inside.

'It isn't far. I've got myself a comfortable little cabin in what's left of the woods,' Poverty Joe said. 'Plenty private. Good liquor on hand, too, though I'm not a noisy tippler like the desperadoes down there.'

Downslope sounds of merriment came from the best one of the conglomeration of ramshackle clapboard buildings that had once housed the mine's administration. Lamplight shone through the broken windows.

'I happen to know Skann's boys have gotten three stolen, five-gallon barrels of whiskey to work through.'

Joshua was pleased to hear it. Maybe they'd be happily insensible to the mine itself. Any notion their prisoner might be set free to escape wouldn't cross their intoxicated minds until it was way too late.

Poverty's thoughts apparently ran along similar lines. 'Hah! When the cats are minded to come back to play, they'll find their mouse has gone.'

The starkness of the mine company lot, its structures a grey ghostliness in the moonlight, gave way to where a horse was picketed behind the concealment of a heap of detritus grown high with tough weeds.

'We don't have far to go. The nag will

carry double no trouble,' Poverty said.

But the ride was not an easy one and Joshua closed his eyes, finding it helped him keep his seat in a reeling world where the clop of the horse's hoofs was like hammer blows in his skull.

And there were new questions to niggle at his befuddled wits.

Who was this Poverty Joe? Was he entirely right in the head? He struck Joshua as being different from the normal run of eccentric loners he'd met, if not actually crazy.

What was his interest in the Skann gang and why was he disposed to freeing its captive? Why did he have such a secretive manner? What was he doing — holed up, it sounded — in a cabin in some woods?

Was there a dark reason why he should take Joshua there rather than on to the town of Silverville?

It was all damned odd, Joshua decided. Good Samaritans existed for sure, yet he had a hunch this one came with underlying motives.

But hell, Poverty Joe was probably all right. Anyway, the condition Joshua was in, going along with the fellow to his cabin suited fine. Tomorrow he could always shift right on out . . .

Or could he?

6

Striking Gold

The code of the West was that you didn't pry into a man's past. Flights to the frontier were often motivated by the desire to start over and be done with an inconvenient past. Better than most, a former Pinkerton detective knew prudence advocated no unmannerly questioning of those who hitched up with you, especially if they'd done you vital service. Like rescued you from an outlaw bunch.

'The nearest doc is down to Silverville, of course, and he charges fierce as a wounded bull,' Poverty Joe told Joshua. 'He'd've advised bed rest for a case like yours. And it's been no problem to give you bunk space here, without a bill to foot. To be honest, I've welcomed a spell of company.'

81

'Here' was Poverty's cabin, a rough and ready but comfortable abode set high on a ridge, in an unlogged stand of sombre pines that constantly whispered in the wind. Built of stone and log, the cabin had two rooms and a brush-thatched lean-to. Poverty had, in fact, given up the one bunk to his guest and slept in a shake-down on the floor. That was when he wasn't dozing in a cane-bottom chair, reading a book or sipping expensive imported whiskey. The cabin had a surprisingly ample supply of both commodities. Poverty Joe had to be a misnomer.

Joshua had interrupted what looked like the life of a cagey drunk, scholar and recluse for three days while his state of health had steadily improved to the point where he felt in reasonable command of his faculties, if not champing at the bit to resume his interrupted mission.

Also, unless Joshua was reading him wrong, Poverty had some undeclared interest in learning his, Joshua's, business and how it had brought him up against Cord Skann and his gang.

'What were you saying about why you were riding to Silverville?' Poverty probed.

As far as Joshua recalled, he hadn't said a word, but maybe a little information would lead to a trade.

'I'm a man who makes inquiries for folks. A city lady in Denver commissioned me to make some in Silverville.'

'What about?' Poverty said, nothing if not blunt.

Joshua studied him. In the moment's silence, he saw what he knew he was supposed to see: a mountain rat, an old prospector retired or disappointed, a drunken hermit. The Rockies had a fair sprinkling of them.

'You could say it was a family matter, to do with a deceased man's will at bottom.'

'Hah! Troublesome affairs, wills.'

'You have experience?'

'Who, me? Why no, sir. Closest I come to willed money is my Silverville friends, the Bennett household.'

This would have knocked Joshua back on his heels if he'd been standing. It seemed akin to a lucky gold strike, a stretching of coincidence. And hadn't that also been the case when Poverty was on hand to rescue him from Cord Skann and his gang?

He gulped. Said, 'These people are wealthy by inheritance?'

'Mrs Bennett's husband lived a very productive business life in Denver and built his fortunes well. Honouring him, so to speak, she continues to build on them in Silverville.'

'How do you know her?'

'Oh, well enough,' Poverty said airily. 'I do chores for the household and that brings me handy whiskey money. Also, they let me play the piano there — I do miss piano-playing — and I have long palavers with the other Joe on the place, a Joseph Darcy.'

Joshua listened with disbelief. He controlled a sense of growing excitement. This was the first break he'd been given in what had till now seemed an ill-fated mission. A source of information had been just about thrown in his lap!

Near breathless, he said, 'How does he fit in — this Joe Darcy?'

Poverty chuckled secretively. 'Mr Joseph Darcy to the world,' he corrected. 'An admirable fellow, Mr Darcy. Smart. Experienced. Always has heaps to talk about with a want-to-know-it-all like me. I have to profess deep admiration for him. He was the late Mr Bennett's private secretary and now he serves his widow in the same capacity. They're making pots of money.'

'Is that all?' Joshua dared to ask.

'What do you mean?'

'Well, it sounded from what you said they live under the same roof and I wondered if they — uh — had more than a business association.'

'Jennie — that is, Mrs Bennett — is a young woman in her prime. Mr Darcy considers her very lovely, I'm sure, and she certainly relies upon him.'

Joshua decided it would pay to show his cards.

'Poverty, I have to be honest with you. What you're telling me is a huge stroke of luck. I was headed to Silverville to visit with these very people. You see, my client, the lady in Denver, is Mrs Bennett's sister-in-law. She's paying me to investigate the murder of her brother — to uncover overlooked clues, trace his killer and bring the person or persons to justice.'

He didn't think it would be politic to further reveal that Flora Bennett was hinting Jennie Bennett and Joseph Darcy might have been part of a conspiracy to eliminate Ryan Bennett.

Poverty Joe nodded slowly, thoughtfully.

'How about that?' he said at length. 'Mighty interesting, but what do I have to do with it? And where's your luck?'

Joshua said, 'If you were to introduce me to your friends it might help, mightn't it? It's a tolerable delicate business, securing a widow's permission to talk to her about her husband's death, reviving memories of the horror. You have to consider that in this case the poor fellow's head was blown off with a shotgun.'

'So you want me to use my good standing to try to ease you in.'

'That's about it. You'd be doing Mrs Bennett a big favour if I can prompt her to recall something that wasn't asked or has been forgotten by the regular law enforcers. I'm a widower myself and I know how the loss hurts and keeps right on a-hurting. I'll do it gently. Considerately . . . '

Joshua knew he was being deceitful, not about the permanent hurt in his own heart, but because his real intention was to check out the possibility that Poverty Joe's friends were murderers.

Poverty Joe contemplated, then drew a deep breath and nodded.

'All right. I'll go into town and fix it for you, Joshua. But I'll have to warn them you're an inquiry agent. It'll be up to Mrs Bennett and Mr Darcy whether they consent to any meeting.'

Though the response was co-operative, the firm note of willingness in Poverty's voice was forced.

'That's reasonable,' Joshua said.

The preparations were made; two days later, Joshua was back on the road to Silverville, having borrowed Poverty's horse.

* * *

Out of caution, Poverty Joe had directed Joshua on to a lesser trail than the main road from Denver. It was possible Cord Skann and his gang of squatting desperadoes hadn't given up on the hope of recapturing their escaped prisoner.

'What about yourself?' Joshua had asked. 'I don't like to leave you here with no means to ride out.'

'I've got a pack mule, haven't I?' Poverty had reminded him. 'Anyways, I'm used to living lonesome now. The

Skann gang hasn't bothered me yet, and has no reason to suspect my interference, though they know I side with the Bennett faction in Silverville.'

The devious, unmarked route Poverty had recommended to Joshua made for a rugged journey along the sides of steep, timbered slopes. Sometimes he found the horse just about stepping on the tops of pines and dwarf oaks lower than the trail. Eruptions of bare rock were obstacles that forced the path to twist and turn so it gave an illusion of doubling back on itself.

Once, the horse, which knew the way, hesitated and Joshua reined it on to a vague, false trail. It proved no more than the track beaten by a foraging bear and descended to a dead end in a cherry grove.

The nearby presence of the grizzly had, of course, been the reason for the horse's reluctance to proceed. Brown bears were creatures of insatiable appetite. This one, feeding on the cherries, was no exception. When they came upon it, the horse balked fearfully at the sight of the wild animal — a full-grown specimen probably about six years old, shaggy and brown with a collar of lighter hair.

Joshua knew that bear attacks on men were rare unless the hairy beasts were cornered, injured or provoked by dogs. Even so, and though he wasn't surprised by its retreat, he was thankful when the bear promptly fled the scene of its disturbed meal, crashing through brush, growling disapproval.

It was the ride's only encounter.

On arrival, Joshua found downtown Silverville largely a single potholed main street. Some narrower, switchback streets branched off the thoroughfare, rising steeply to benches a full thousand yards up the sloping, valley sides which enclosed the noise and bustle like solid walls of rock.

The town crowded along the main street and valley floor included three hotels, two restaurants, about thirty stores or warehouses, a bakery, a laundry, mills and smelters.

The latter filled the air with continuous hubbub and smoky fumes from belching chimney stacks.

Many men, but a lesser number of women, walked or rode the street. They were of all races. The Orientals were especially apparent. The Chinamen, as they were invariably classed, wore caps and robes, smocks and slippers and glided swiftly and purposefully about their business, be it in restaurant, gambling den or laundry.

Outside a saloon, two dishevelled miners in faded blue shirts and clay-stained boots engaged in vociferous dickering with each other and a brightly dressed, hard-faced woman in an ostrich-feathered hat.

'Come on then, gents! Whichever of yuh's got five dollars,' the woman screeched. 'Won't bother me, I'm sure. But fer both at once, it'll be fifteen!'

'That'll be a shameful price indeed,' one of the men complained.

The woman laughed raucously. 'Mebbe

it's fer a shameful doin'!'

There didn't look to be much peace in this valley. The best that could be said for it was that to a visitor passing through it might appear picturesque. For a grieving widow seeking refuge from a cruel world, it looked about as fitting as the pit of Acheron. It was likely one of the wildest towns in America. Full of money and overt sin if Joshua knew anything of such places.

What made it a desirable abode for Jennie Bennett?

Of course, it could be the financial opportunities. Flora Bennett had told him how her brother's fortune had been reinvested in the place, to the extent that a large percentage of all money made here now found its way into the Bennett coffers. Whether this made it necessary for Jennie Bennett to be on the spot was open to conjecture, but he could understand how the hand on the tiller — and the tills — might need to be present. And that hand was reportedly Joseph Darcy's.

Maybe Jennie saw her place as being at his side . . .

How closely at his side he was shortly to discover.

★   ★   ★

He directed his mount up one of the sloping side streets. The animal seemed familiar with the way and the house that dominated the clifftop it gave access to was clearly the grandest in the valley. To begin with, it was painted and gable-ended, looking somewhat in the style of a Swiss chalet.

Once reached, the Bennett mansion's position didn't strike Joshua as so precarious. It was backed by a thick belt of pines that from below had made it look like it was about to be crowded off its high perch. Close up, he saw that an ample girdle of lawn and shrubbery divided the house from both the trees and the precipice to the front. It could almost have been artistically arranged by a landscape gardener, but he figured the house site had simply been chosen and paid for well. It had an atmosphere of wealth and aloofness.

He tugged just once on the bell-pull at the porticoed front entrance.

No one answered the summons. The property seemed silent; shut up.

Joshua checked his watch. Yeah, maybe he was a few minutes early . . .

He listened again. Was that a sound of life back of the house? He could easily check. He took himself with care up the steep, grassed slope and slipped among the pine boles at the crest.

Looking back through the screening trees, he could see in the rear windows of the Bennett residence. One room had an expensively large expanse of glass, and the drapes were not drawn. Moreover, the windows were open and to his ears drifted a woman's soft moaning.

But more arresting and fascinating was what he saw.

Though he wasn't the type to indulge in voyeurism, he froze into immobility and momentarily stared.

Items of clothing were scattered across the carpeted floor of the room he overlooked from door to four-poster bed. They included a pair of men's pants, longjohns — unbuttoned only sufficiently to allow removal — a woman's corset trailing loosened lacing, and lawn drawers trimmed with lace and embroidered red flowers.

In itself, an interesting trail, which ended between the bed's posters. The end of the bed faced the window and the uncaring trees outside. All that was really visible to Joshua was the woman's pretty knees raised either side of the man's back.

Joshua guessed the couple were insensible to the passage of time. He wasted none himself in retreating surreptitiously back to the front porch.

He jangled the bell again.

This time he waited.

Waited and waited, it seemed. Patience was easier achieved than control of his racing pulses and envy. It was hard to put the glimpsed images and sounds out of his mind.

He thought he heard shuffling and scurrying within the house but couldn't be sure.

Finally, the door opened.

7

The Ungrieving Widow

'Oh, how silly of me! I gave the servants the afternoon off and quite forgot we were expecting a guest.'

The young woman who opened the door to Joshua, smiling a welcome, looked to be in her late twenties and was of medium, delightful build. Befitting a recent widow, she wore a modestly cut, high-collared black dress, but the bodice moulded itself to her figure, unintentionally drawing attention to her charms rather than concealing them. The fabric was taut across a slightly heaving bosom, snug at the waist and only full in the skirt.

Also, she'd missed fastening the second button from the neck, and her honey-blonde hair, though pinned up, looked a little mussed, as though she'd attended to it hurriedly. And her cheeks were flushed.

Joshua didn't doubt the reason for her less than perfect grooming or her high colour. He guessed she was both Mrs Jennie Bennett and the woman he'd seen minutes earlier with a lover.

But he hadn't glimpsed much more, then, than shapely legs, so he didn't know it. A gentleman could scarcely ask a lady to raise her skirts: 'Ma'am, I think I saw you just now. Could you please show me your knees?'

She gushed on, her words coming in a nervous flood. She was very feminine, effervescent, somehow mettlesome, like a partly broke mare. Damned pretty . . . Joshua couldn't help but categorize her as the type who would make love uncomplicatedly and passionately.

She was personable and therefore someone who probably would be widely and readily liked.

'I'm Mrs Bennett,' she confirmed, 'and you must be Mr Dillard, I presume. So sorry to keep you at the door. I don't know why I didn't keep an eye on the clock!'

Joshua wondered if it would put her in even more of a fluster if he told her he did know.

'Yes, ma'am, I'm Dillard — Joshua Dillard. A pleasure to meet you. And the wait was just fine. I was some early.'

'Do come in.'

She ushered him into a luxuriously furnished yet comfortable front parlour. It was a large room with a lofty, plastered ceiling. Gilt-framed paintings were on the walls and the windows were artistically draped with rich red and gold curtains.

A piano occupied one corner, a pile of song sheets on the stool.

'I must apologize for intruding at a time I'm sure your grief is still powerfully with you,' Joshua lied.

She stood just within the doorway, one hand braced on a finely crafted whatnot on which stood a vase of flowers, the fresh blooms pink and blue and beautifully arranged.

'Oh, yes . . . of course,' she said, as though the proper gravity of her situation had only just occurred to her. Then, very soberly, choosing her words carefully, she said, 'I understand you want to ask me some questions about — that.'

Joshua nodded. 'If it wouldn't be too distressing . . . '

'Not at all — I mean, yes, but . . . Listen, Mr Dillard, before we begin, may I call my . . . secretary?' The hesitation before 'secretary' was a split-second. 'He was Ryan's man and I kept him on. He was also present on that dreadful night and knows just as much as me.'

She licked her lips as though summoning courage. 'In fact, I insist he helps me with every answer I give.'

Joshua said, 'Why, yes, ma'am. I would have no objection at all. I'm sure it will be helpful.'

She turned and called a summons which sounded like it was going to be a familiar name but was quickly bitten back and became something else preceded by an honorific.

'Mr Darcy! A moment or two, please!'

Joshua was more than happy to meet Joseph Darcy, the shrewd secretary who Flora Bennett believed was the architect of the rapid and successful transferral of her brother's business empire to Silverville.

The man who came in answer to the call was a solidly built gent of commanding appearance with an impressive head of black hair. With some trimming of his full beard and moustache, he might have borne a passing similarity to General Ulysses S. Grant.

Unquestionably, Joshua recognized him as the one whose back he'd seen through the bedroom window — the male half of a couple joined and transported by bliss, not knowing that a stranger had stumbled across a view of it through a window.

Jennie introduced them and hands were shaken.

Joshua felt uncomfortable, aware that

the flesh the hand holding his had last pressed had been female, soft and yielding.

'Honoured to make your acquaintance, Mr Darcy,' he said. 'I've heard much about your recent achievements in Silverville.'

'I do my job, Mr Dillard.'

Jennie Bennett gave Darcy an upwards, sidelong, proud glance. 'And more!'

Joshua was startled for a second. What was she about to confide their intimacy?

She continued in her bubbly manner, 'Mr Darcy is figuring to buy up Silverville's only newspaper. We already own the best mines, a brewery and a gambling hall. And we have mortgages over many other properties. We plan one day to build an opera house, would you believe!'

'It might be beyond most folks' dreaming,' Joshua conceded, 'but seeing what has been achieved already, I expect to see it in due course.'

'Good,' Darcy said. 'I'm always in

accord with a man who expects what to most might be unexpected.'

'However,' Jennie said, 'opera houses notwithstanding, we will be protecting our privacy here. The crime you wish to discuss closed the Denver chapter of my life for good. I don't choose to be subjected to the bright lights of society and popular speculation any more.'

Darcy said, 'That's right. Ask your questions if you must, Mr Dillard, but Mrs Bennett can tell nothing that isn't already known. I will warn you now, this appointment will be your one chance. You'll be permitted to make no continuing nuisance of yourself, sir.'

Joshua mentally accepted that Darcy had been Ryan Bennett's financial adviser and business manager, that the role had survived his boss's death, but his warning sounded a mite high-handed coming from an employee. What he'd seen in the bedroom, and Darcy's protectiveness toward Jennie, struck him as out of keeping with their situation as it was presented to the world.

'Well, the crime was tolerable infamous in Denver,' he said. 'I'd admire to be of assistance to Mr Bennett's distressed sister. She commissioned me in the hope I'd track down the murderer — now suspected to be one Zach Skann, who has vanished from all sight.'

'Ah, yes, Zach Skann,' Darcy said smoothly. 'A blackguard eaten up by considerable anger and error who had made his threats known in criminal circles. His brother, Cord, an outlaw type of similar notoriety, has shown up here lately to bother Mrs Bennett and myself with wild and unfounded claims. Besmirching our reputation in low saloons and other dens of iniquity which the silver-boom communities sadly attract. I'll stand for no suchlike talk from a gentleman such as yourself!'

Joshua realized it was going to be a delicate, difficult business interviewing the pair.

He ran over the broad details of what had been reported in the Denver press about Ryan Bennett's demise. For once, it seemed, the newspapermen had not sensationalized.

An apparent robber, armed with a shotgun, had broken in on them at the Capitol Hill house while Jennie had been singing. Rye and Joseph had resisted his demands and tried to overpower him. A struggle had developed and the gun had been discharged, killing Rye.

Latterly, Joshua repeated, it had been suggested the intruder was Zach Skann. Rye Bennett had been his nemesis in a past time, when he'd worked as a Pinkerton detective. He'd come seeking retribution and it had been his intention all along to blow Bennett away.

While Jennie and Joseph had been overcome with horror at the gruesome slaying, Skann had fled the house. He hadn't been seen in Denver again.

'The newspaper reports were largely accurate, Mr Dillard.'

'We can add little . . . '

'It was enormously distressing. I'm

sure you understand.'

Joshua thought better of bringing Flora Bennett's interpretation of the events to the attention of Jennie and Darcy. Whatever he might get out of this conversation would be what they wanted him to get, and that would be almighty little.

Evidently, he was not going to be allowed to question Jennie alone — and on some points she was nervy and vague.

'Others involved? No, I don't think we saw anybody. Could there have been?'

And, 'I don't understand. Surely you've been told nothing of that sort. But I don't know. Could it be possible?'

Deliberately vague, or taking refuge in the knowledge only a cad would revive her distress with an insistence on detailed recall of everything that took place on a fateful night?

Moreover, the pair of them exchanged long and meaningful glances at certain crucial junctures, speaking to each other with their eyes, as only lovers — and maybe co-conspirators — did.

Joshua was confounded.

Flora was right on one count: Jennie was Darcy's woman now, before her husband was properly cold in his grave. But had she been Darcy's woman even before Bennett's death, and had they masterminded it?

Were Darcy and Jennie Ryan Bennett's real murderers?

He made a suggestion, trying to make it sound casual but failing.

'Miss Flora Bennett is still very put out by the mystery surrounding her brother's death. Couldn't you go visit with her in Denver, or invite her here? Put her mind at rest?'

Darcy snapped, 'No mystery really, except Zach Skann has been allowed to escape. That should have taught some to expect the unexpected! So completely has he vanished that his own brother is hounding us here, spreading malicious rumours.'

Jennie was more quietly adamant.

'I don't think it would be a good idea for us to see Flora. Our paths had best never cross again. It would bring back too many painful memories. Besides, Miss Bennett never approved of Mr Darcy, even when he was Ryan's secretary. As I said, the Denver chapter of my life is closed for good.'

'Will that be all, Mr Dillard?' Darcy said.

Joshua's time was up; his visit over. Darcy had decided.

Joshua sighed. 'I guess so, Mr Darcy. Thank you, both. I'll be on my way.'

★   ★   ★

All in all, the call at the Bennett house hadn't gone too badly, if it hadn't gone well. He had some firsthand facts gathered by questioning and personal observation, albeit the latter had been partly luck and made him feel as though he'd been a peeper. Thank God he hadn't been caught.

Joshua hied himself into Silverville.

108

He weaved through the boom-town's crowds before finally doubling back to the quietest of the saloons, the Miners' Rest, to take stock over a beer at a corner table. It wasn't the best drink he'd tasted, nor the worst, but it was cool and that by itself was refreshing.

Jennie Bennett and Joseph Darcy were indeed more than employer and employee. He had no doubt they were very affectionately disposed to one another. He was now as certain as the incomplete view he'd had would allow that the woman abed with Joseph Darcy had been the fairly recent widow.

He wondered what he should report to Miss Flora Bennett; if he should send preliminary word to Denver that the evidence so far tended to support the damning construction she'd placed on the relationship and actions of her sister-in-law and her brother's secretary.

Several days had already been wasted, due to the attack on himself by Cord Skann's henchmen. Skann, like Flora, reckoned there were good reasons for mounting a watch on Jennie and Darcy.

Flora would be expecting to hear from him, but he was in an awkward position. He was by no means sure he'd be able to prove anything where others had failed. The case was regarded as an open-and-shut affair: all that had to be determined was the whereabouts of the man who'd blasted Bennett to death.

Maybe Flora's assumptions of a Machiavellian plot were moonshine — hogwash — anyway. Had he gotten involved with the matter from a wrong angle? Flora wanted money, like most everyone, but maybe she was after more. Greed fed greed. Her real motive might purely be the destruction of her sister-in-law and the happiness she was apparently seeking with a new lover.

Unless Flora received her bequest, Joshua would be out of pocket — a situation very familiar but not acceptable on any grounds. It was also unlikely any other promised reward would be forthcoming.

He took another deep swallow of the near-flavourless beer. Appears you've picked another dud assignment, Joshua Dillard, he admonished silently.

The saloon was only scantily patronized and Joshua became aware that two men were taking an interest in him. It ranged from swift glances to calculated stares.

Joshua toyed with his half-emptied glass. He was a stranger in town, but a place like Silverville must attract plenty of newcomers. Then one of the two men, who'd been dealing each other poker hands at a far table near the batwing doors, carefully put down his cards.

He went to the bar, leaned on the mahogany and spoke questioningly to the keeper. He made a kind of half-nod toward Joshua. The barman put down the glass he was polishing on the back bar, ran hands nervously down his stained apron and shook his head.

Nope, he doesn't know me, Joshua thought.

The card player swept the room with a gaze that was a mite too nonchalant to be innocent but allowed for a further quick appraisal of Joshua. After that, he returned to his table, spoke briefly to his companion, and slipped out through the batwings.

Now what?

Joshua didn't have long to wait. Within minutes, the card player returned with a couple of folded bills in his hand and accompanied. He looked over to the nervy barkeep with a self-congratulatory smirk on his face, as though to say 'I was right.'

The face that pushed in behind him was grimmer — large-nosed, beard-stubbled, framed by straggly black hair. And it was dark with anger and frustration.

Breathing hard, like he'd hurried, the new arrival stormed across the sawdusted floor, heading straight for Joshua.

Cord Skann.

8

Gun Trouble

'So you've gotten here, huh?' Skann said.

'Yeah, I'm here, but no thanks to you.'

'You seen Jennie Bennett and Joe Darcy?'

'What if I have?'

'Answer the question, damn you!'

'Don't take that tone with me, Skann! You might be cock of the walk when just your bully-boys are around, but it don't wash here. Fact is, seeing you're in town, I've a mind to swear out a complaint against you at the marshal's office.'

'On account of what?'

'On account of a shot horse, abduction and being held against my will.'

Skann sneered. 'My heart bleeds, Dillard, but you'll be wastin' your time, an' I figure you know it, bein' a clever dick an' all. The Maybelline mine is both outside town limits an' Charley Broadstreet's jurisdiction.'

Joshua pursed his lips. He said, 'What do you want, and why?'

Skann's eyes glittered with malice. They said he wanted nothing better than to smash his big, clenched fists into Joshua's face.

'I want to *know*. You heard the question, Dillard! Have you seen the Bennett widow an' her fancy-man?'

Across the bar-room, someone else had come through the batwings. The glance Joshua caught was enough to make him look again, realizing who the figure was.

The eccentric hobo could be none other: Poverty Joe had come to town for some reason.

Joshua said to Skann without a further flicker, 'If you were listening, you'd've gathered I wanted to be told what it is to you who I call on.'

Skann growled, 'You want me to talk plainer? I say you seen 'em. An' by now you'll be in cahoots with 'em. I know how high-toned trash handle Pinkerton scum. They'll've bought you off, like they buy e'ry goddamned thing else! They killed Rye Bennett theirselves an' framed my brother — forced him inta hidin', run him outa the country! Darcy's a dirty dog an' the pretty widow-woman is his whore!'

Poverty Joe's cry rang out among the murmurs Skann's accusations excited from the small crowd that listened agog.

'You're a lying rat, Cord Skann! All the town is indebted to Mrs Bennett and Darcy. It knows they're good people!'

A savage snarl broke from between Skann's lips as he spun round.

'Too much of the town is in their pocket to say much other! An' fer why else are they buyin' up the newspaper 'cept to get control of what it prints!'

The other patrons around Poverty Joe edged back from him, leaving him exposed. But he was a plucky rooster and wasn't about to back down.

'More filthy lies, Skann! You and your troublemakers are stirring trouble hereabouts. You're waging a campaign to disrupt the Bennett businesses!'

Joshua knew on Cord Skann's own admission he was all outlaw. He didn't raise hell in the cause of worker justice, like his brother supposedly had. Poverty Joe knew it, too. He'd told Joshua that Skann was a gunfighter with a reputation. Down his back-trail men had fallen, beaten by his fast draw. What the hell was Poverty thinking of, aggravating him like this?

Skann said, 'You got a big mouth an' a lotta nerve, mister! No man calls me a liar and don't take it back fast. Less you get down on your knees an' kiss my boots, I'm gonna shoot your kneecaps off, bust your legs an' leave you a gimp!'

Joshua knew he had it in him to carry

out his threat. This Skann was barely more sane than men he'd seen incarcerated in state lunatic hospitals.

With Skann's attention diverted, he drew his Colt Peacemaker and cocked it. 'Is that a fact, Mr Skann?'

'Hold it, gents!' blurted the agitated barkeep, lifting his hands. 'There'll be no gunplay in these premises!'

Skann *laughed*.

'Ain't gonna be, slops mopper! Leastways, not in any wise this Pinkerton bastard thinks. See, two of my pals just slid in behind him through your back door. He'll put his gun away. Then we'll make a regular thing of it — see who draws an' fires fastest.'

Joshua turned his head fractionally. To his shock and self-disgust, his glance told him Skann was pulling no ruse. Squint-eyed Virg and the humourless Slim were there, covering him with drawn pistols.

Try anything and he wouldn't have a prayer. Or would he?

He shrugged his shoulders, lowered

his gun and with his left hand picked up the half-empty glass of watery beer in front of him.

But somehow he dropped the glass before it reached his lips. The fumble was distractingly natural, and the apparent accident baffled all watchers' eyes. It looked like he was trying to catch the glass, till with greased swiftness he rolled under the table, turning it on its side, and putting its solid top between him and Skann.

In the same instant, the Peacemaker in his right hand crashed. Flame flashed from the blued-steel muzzle.

Slim's pistol exploded as it flew from his nerveless hand. Joshua's trick shot from the floor had broken his gun arm. He squealed.

Virg's crossed eyes met Joshua's, light blue and glittering like ice. Joshua's smoking six-gun spoke with menace that he backed with words.

'Drop it — or next time I pull trigger, I shoot to kill!'

Virg switched his startled, crooked

gaze, presumably to his boss, seeking instruction. 'Hell, Slim's been shot!'

Skann roared, 'I'll take him myself, you fool!'

But another voice said, 'There'll be no back-shooting, Skann!'

It was Poverty Joe who'd hauled a Remington piece from a shoulder holster.

'Damn your hide, whisker-face!' Skann said, swinging his weapon.

And the deafening crash of gunplay rocked the Miners' Rest.

As gaping onlookers tried to squeeze out of all possible lines of fire, Poverty and Skann exchanged hasty shots. Poverty missed. Skann did not.

Simultaneously, Virg found his courage but had already lost his chance. Joshua rolled again, escaping the bullet that drilled the floorboards where he'd been crouched, putting one of his own bloodily in Virg's shoulder.

This was scary business. People who hadn't been sure what to do were now leaving fast.

'They'll wreck the place — kill us all!' the barkeep said. 'Fetch the marshal!'

The cry wasn't necessary. The sound of gunfire had already done the job. Outside, voices were raised in excited speculation and hurrying, booted feet pounded on the plank walk. Two men armed with shotguns and with tin stars on their coats rushed into the saloon, pushing through the small stampede of bodies quitting. Patrons who got in their way were moved aside with meaty thumps from the guns' stocks.

Skann didn't stick around to run foul of the marshal, his deputy or their scatterguns. He took a run, a jump on to a table and, raising an arm to shield his face, smashed his heavy-boned body shoulder-first into the saloon's front window. Glass crashed; framing splintered. He booted out some jutting shards, leaped through the wreckage and was gone.

The deputy yelled, 'Hold it!'

But no one tried to stop him. You'd

have needed a big interest in the ruckus to be that brave. And in a moderately crowded town situation short of riot, the lawmen's murderous but undiscriminating shotguns served best as clubs.

The deputy let Skann go.

'You know who I am?' the elder lawman asked, standing over Joshua.

'No, I don't believe I do.'

The man tapped his star. 'Marshal Charley Broadstreet.'

He was a middle-aged man in a neat brown suit and a flat-crowned, wide-brimmed tan hat. His face was patrician and the way he spoke reminded Joshua of a sternly mannered schoolmaster, but with his shotgun he probably terrorized the drunks on a Saturday night.

His eyes flicked over the damage, taking in the spilled furniture, the smashed glassware and the three men with bullet wounds.

'I'll take the guns.'

Joshua handed over his Peacemaker.

The deputy kicked Virg, Slim and Poverty Joe's guns, which were on the floor, into a heap.

Poverty Joe was prone and barely conscious. The deputy crouched and examined him.

'Will he live?' Broadstreet asked.

'He's hit in the lower part of the chest. Hit a rib and comed out the side, looks like. He's in powerful bad shape but stop the bleeding and maybe he'll pull through.'

'Organize taking him to Doc Pike's,' Broadstreet ordered the shaking barkeeper. 'Carry him on a door or something.' Then to Virg and Slim, 'You two and him,' nodding to Joshua, 'are headed to the jail-house to cool off.'

'We're bleedin', too!' Slim complained. 'What about doctorin' fer us?'

'You ain't so bad you'll die,' Broadstreet said dismissively. 'A few little old scratches can be patched up in a cell. The doc might see you later.'

He turned his attention to Joshua's gun. He sniffed at the muzzle and broke it open to examine the chambers.

'You shoot these men?'

'The two of 'em standing. In self-defence, Marshal: shoot or be shot myself.'

'I didn't ask why, mister. This isn't time nor place to have your say. You'll wait some, understand? I don't do questioning in saloons — just restoring the peace.'

'I don't need questioning. I'll make a statement, then I'd like my gun back.'

But Broadstreet meant to keep order his way and wasn't about to be persuaded by any stranger's arguments.

'You'll get it back when it pleases me. And sure, you'll make a statement. Else it's satisfactory, you'll stay locked up till the case can go before a judge. Same if one of the other gents swears out a complaint.'

Joshua felt exasperated; the marshal wasn't kidding. He indicated Virg and Slim with a derogatory sweep of his hand.

'But these men — these *gents* — are

outlaws. You've probably got paper on them! I came to Silverville on business. There's no call to hold me in jail.'

'We'll see about that. Who pays for the damages done here? Smashed windows and the like?'

'I can't be blamed for that stuff! There were plenty of witnesses — '

But with bullets flying and the law horning in, the Miners' Rest was emptier than ever. Besides, no one here knew Joshua Dillard except Poverty Joe, who wasn't in a fit state to talk. Joshua was also keenly aware he'd avoided putting even Poverty in the picture completely.

Broadstreet stood firm. He spoke with the world-weariness of a peace officer who'd seen and heard all the protests of the unruly before. Gunplay in a saloon was no extraordinary turn of events for a Colorado mining district.

It was a hard, tough life lawdogging in a place like Silverville. Joshua had briefly, memorably experienced being a mining-town marshal in Montana, which helped him to understand that. And to know that Broadstreet was hard and tough, too . . .

'I told you we'd see, didn't I?' Broadstreet said. 'You ain't hurt. I'm taking you in. Start walking, mister — out the doors and turn left!'

9

Words with the Marshal

The Silverville hoosegow was built of stone and kept clean to the point of clinical. Joshua was learning more about Marshal Charley Broadstreet every moment. He ran an orderly operation. Hard and unyielding he might be, but Joshua figured that by taking Broadstreet's curtailment of his freedom calmly, and replying to his questions honestly, he could turn the sorry incident in the saloon to his advantage.

Broadstreet was the breed of lawman who'd have a finger on the pulse of his town.

A half-hour later, Joshua sat in an iron-barred cell on the edge of a wooden bunk stacked with neatly folded blankets and told his story. The cell was comparatively private, though when their voices were raised in complaint, Joshua recognized that Skann's Slim and Virg were held in a part of the same block but out of his line of sight and proper hearing.

Broadstreet asked, 'This a personal thing with the Skann bunch?'

Joshua told him no, it hadn't started that way; how he'd come to town to speak to Mrs Jennie Bennett and her secretary, Joseph Darcy, on behalf of the late Mr Bennett's sister who wanted to reach a conclusion about the vengeance killing of her brother by Zach Skann.

He told how he'd been waylaid by Cord Skann's men and held briefly prisoner till he'd been rescued by Poverty Joe.

'I hope the poor feller hasn't thrown away his life, protecting the honour of Mrs Bennett and Darcy, whose reputations were being tarnished by Cord Skann in the Miners' Rest.'

Broadstreet said, 'The doc declares he'll survive, but he lost considerable blood. The advice is for bedrest at the doc's place. He runs a kind of small hospital.' Then he revealed, 'Mrs Bennett has already sent word through Mr Darcy that she'll pay the doc's bills in full. Nobody in their right mind goes up against the Bennett interests in this town.'

'But Cord Skann isn't in his right mind. I also take it you don't aim to buck Mrs Bennett or Joseph Darcy yourself.'

Broadstreet's eyes narrowed shrewdly. 'I won't take offence at that, Mr Dillard. I'm my own man and the law's man.'

'Glad to hear it. I take it nobody's told you I've already been received by Mrs Bennett and Mr Darcy, up at their grand house.'

This time Broadstreet's eyes widened. 'Well, I am some surprised at that. They make a point to avoid contact with outsiders — 'specially folks from Denver, which you've given as your last place of abode.'

'We met and parted on amicable terms, Marshal.'

Broadstreet reflected on this. He reached in a side pocket of his coat and took out a couple of thin cigars. He handed one to Joshua, who thanked him, said he'd save it for later and pocketed it.

Broadstreet carefully cut off the end of his and lit up.

Joshua said, 'How do you mean, they avoid Denver people?'

'Well,' Broadstreet said between puffs, 'it appears the city has unpleasant memories for them.'

'Which is understandable.'

'Sure, and they do — uh — fuss about it. There was a Fourth-of-July shindig. When some visitors from Denver showed up, the pair quickly made themselves scarce, retreating to the house just about as one.'

Joshua thought nothing was to be gained by either of them beating about the bush.

'Marshal, I'm not minded to conceal

that I know Jennie Bennett and Joseph Darcy are mighty close. Scandalously, some might say, with her husband not too long passed. Maybe that's why they behave oddly. Embarrassment do you think? Guilt?'

Broadstreet eyed him with sharp suspicion. Or it could be renewed hostility.

'That's for neither you nor I to judge.' He jabbed his cigar toward Joshua for emphasis. 'I've said about all I aim to say. I better add, however, that after those unwelcome visitors left, Mrs Bennett and Darcy were discovered hiding in a broom closet. Darcy explained he'd been comforting the lady. He said she'd had an attack of panic at the prospect of coming face to face with people she and her husband had known in Denver.'

Joshua smiled crookedly. He wondered how Broadstreet would react if he said he'd spied Jennie Bennett and Darcy in a situation more compromising than a broom closet. The tidbit of information Broadstreet had imparted was clearly designed to tell him the marshal was no fool; knew what was afoot. He decided not to push his luck.

'What does Silverville say about this?'

'This isn't Denver, Dillard. By and large, Silverville don't care. The few gossips and know-alls interested in the moral niceties suspicion that when a decent spell of mourning has been allowed, Joseph Darcy and his deceased boss's widow will become man and wife. However, most ever'body do say Darcy's a lucky dog, seeing as Jennie Bennett is a real beauty and a rich 'un. All enterprises of note in this town are now Bennett owned. To boot, the estate has mortgages on much of what's left. You don't hear much bad-mouthing.'

'Apart from Cord Skann's,' Joshua said.

Broadstreet took the correction in good part. 'True, but Skann is an outsider, arriving after Mrs Bennett and Mr Darcy took up residence.'

'A man with a grudge.'

'Exactly. Joseph Darcy warned me about how Skann lays blame for his brother's disappearance at the Bennett door. Like as if Ryan Bennett asked to be murdered and obliged Zach to go on the dodge or face a hangrope. Darcy appealed to me, for Mrs Bennett's sake, to drive Skann and his roughnecks out. That ain't easy though. A mining town naturally has a wilder element. It's hard for the lawful authorities to separate individuals from the general populace without arousing animosity and stirring more general disorder.'

Joshua stressed that he had his own argument with Cord Skann.

'Like I said, Skann ambushed me on the road to Silverville. He has it in for the Bennett camp for sure, I know that. Hates the guts of anyone who might have dealings with them, like Poverty Joe. Skann is scum of a breed I can't abide!'

Broadstreet wasn't about to argue. He blew out cigar smoke.

'Truth to tell, Silverville being what it

is draws plenty of scum, but Cord Skann and his pards are the biggest sonsofbitches I seen forking broncs in this neck of the woods. They're a burr under the Silverville saddle. Because this town is a Bennett town — *the* Bennett town nowadays — Skann and his hard-cases are out to cause trouble for most everyone. I was half-ready for shooting like there was in the Miners' Rest. Darcy has told me frequently: always expect the unexpected.'

'Sounds to me Skann is a thorn in everyone's flesh. You going to jail all those who stand up to him or have business with the Bennett faction?'

Joshua had figured Broadstreet knew this would be impractical and ridiculous. Stated outright, the goading brought a response. But it was not yet the one he was angling for — which was to be given back his freedom.

Looking at him squarely through a cloud of exhaled smoke, Broadstreet said, 'You're a disturbing feller, Dillard.'

Joshua said nothing.

Broadstreet weighed his options.

Joshua felt the tension in the air. He could say very little more to help the marshal reach a decision without completely betraying the confidence of his client. It might also be impolitic for him to make plain Flora Bennett's distrust of her sister-in-law and her brother's secretary, who were the powers in Broadstreet's land.

The silence dragged. Broadstreet examined the glowing tip of his smoke.

Joshua was strongly tempted to start speaking, to say anything to break the uneasiness between them. But he forced himself to sit quietly and after a spell, Broadstreet relented.

He crushed out his cigar and said, 'Very well, Dillard. I'm inclined to trust you, and I won't keep you locked up. Just don't do anything to disturb the peace, y'understand?'

'I won't hunt more trouble, but I'll finish my business. Thank you.'

Broadstreet handed him back his Colt revolver, which he'd had tucked in his belt.

'If you want my advice — which I doubt — you'd beat it from Silverville before Skann and his hellions kill you.'

'You've got a couple of 'em in the cells,' Joshua pointed out, getting to his feet.

Broadstreet became grave. 'Yeah, but once you're let out, I have to let those boys out by sun-up tomorrow latest — less you can produce solid evidence that obliges me to do otherwise. That's how it works, you must've figured that. Everybody saw you brought in together after the gunplay.'

'I guess. You're honest about the situation here, I'll say that for you.'

'Why not? There's no percentage for a small-town law office in favouring either side when feuding parties bring in quarrels from other parts. It don't look good. I can say you were all drunk; the ruckus was no more'n the result a lot of empty mouth. But with the Skann trash and you on the loose there's apt to be more trouble.'

135

Joshua patted the holstered Peacemaker. 'Trouble and me are no strangers.'

Not wasting any more time, he lifted a hand and went on through the unlocked cell door, moving smoothly and quickly.

Broadstreet called after him warningly, 'Don't push your luck, Dillard.'

★　★　★

Joshua strode out for his next port of call, comparatively satisfied with the outcome of his brief incarceration by the town's law. Though Joshua sensed Broadstreet might have a darker side, he'd been square with him for now. And he'd given him some significant information that might not otherwise have come his way as promptly.

He headed for the Silverville doctor's place, digesting it while wondering what Broadstreet's own games were in Silverville. He thought he had a fair notion of what was going on in the Bennett case, but no proof yet that he could put before Flora, let alone charges that could lead to arrests and a Denver city court.

Certain aspects of what he'd learned suggested at least one key to the affair was held by Poverty Joe. Already he'd been on the scene twice at crucial junctures to play an intervening role.

To Joshua's mind, the interest he might have to justify this was not adequately explained.

The doctor's house was one of the town's largest and best built, situated between a drug store and an undertaker's parlour on the north side of Main Street. It was positioned to catch the best of the sunlight that defied the mountain topography to enter the deep valley. A neatly lettered shingle beside the door said AMBROSE PIKE, PHYSICIAN.

A bell pealed when Joshua opened the door and went in. Inside the door, another sign by a stairway to an upper floor said HOSPITAL. A mite grand, Joshua thought. A third sign, by an inner door, said WAITING ROOM.

A desk inside the waiting room was unattended. Joshua sat on a well-used settee with broken springs and waited.

A full minute passed before a clatter of hurried footsteps sounded on the stairs. A man came in whom Joshua took to be medico.

Doc Pike was gaunt and old with a lengthy white beard. Small, like a gnome, Joshua thought. He was drying his hands on a white towel. He had long, white fingers. He wore striped suit pants without the coat and the sleeves of his white shirt, though gartered, were also rolled up above bony elbows.

'Heard the bell. Sorry to keep you waiting,' he rapped out briskly. 'I was busy. My nurse quit this hell-hole of a town last week — as any decent woman might — and I'm on my own. What can I do for you?'

'I was just visiting,' Joshua said. 'You have a patient here goes by the name of Poverty Joe. May I see him?'

The little doctor put his head to one

side, like an enquiring bird. He was suspicious.

'I haven't seen you before. You a friend of Poverty Joe?'

'You could say.'

'Do Mrs Bennett and Mr Darcy know you've come here?'

'They know I'm in town. I was visiting with them earlier. On business.'

The doctor sighed wearily. 'Very well then. I suppose it's all right. Follow me.'

'Thank you.'

They climbed the stairs.

'Your friend is a critically weak man,' Pike said. 'The bullet hit a rib, breaking it and ripping on through flesh and out the back. He has lost blood.'

Poverty Joe lay on a bed in a room that reeked of carbolic. His face was as white as the pillow beneath his head. His chest was strapped up like a mummy's and padded heavily on one side. But he was conscious. The glint in his eye was feverish.

'Joshua! Tell this old fool of a

sawbones I'll be fine, will you? I've got to get out of here. Cord Skann broke away, I hear. Somebody has to keep an eye out in behalf of Jennie and her — Mr Darcy. He fixes to kill 'em both, I know!'

'Now don't get yourself worked up!' Pike said. 'You'll open up the wound and more of your life's blood will be lost!'

'See here, Pike, I feel better already — '

'You don't look it, man! It'd be a dereliction of medical duty to deny your condition worries me.'

Joshua said, 'Leave me with him, Doc. Maybe if I could have a quiet, private talk, it'll sort out some stuff.'

But Joshua suspected he was telling less than the truth, possibly the reverse of it.

10

Fire in the Blood

'I swear to God nothing you can say will keep me in this bed, Joshua Dillard,' Poverty Joe said.

Doc Pike shrugged and tutted, but he scurried off to other business, bitterly repeating his complaint about the impossibility of hiring nursing staff on a frontier where the few good women were subject to repeated harassment by unmannered males.

Joshua was free to put his questions to Poverty Joe, but the whiskered eccentric was wholly uncooperative.

'I take it your friendship with Mrs Bennett and Joe Darcy predates your spell in Silverville. Did you know them in Denver?'

There was no direct reply.

'I'm mighty appreciative you took my

part in the Miners' Rest,' Poverty said. 'But it's a way back since I admired to talk about life in other places, and now isn't a fitting time at all.'

Joshua persisted, taking another line. 'Did you know Ryan Bennett?'

'Not saying I did; not saying I didn't,' the bandaged man said stubbornly, his face a whiter shade of pale if that was possible.

Joshua began to feel more than a fool. Delving into a man's past was against the code of the West. Men took new names; began new lives. No one denied them their second chance. Asking questions about a stranger or sometimes a friend's privacy wasn't done and was disrespectful.

'I can see you want to volunteer nothing,' Joshua fumed. 'I tell you, I've everyone's best interests in mind here, except those of Cord Skann and his boys.'

He sensed that Poverty Joe was keeping the facts back from him — maybe a lot of facts. It couldn't be put down just to weak-headedness from his loss of blood, he was being obstructive.

Poverty sucked breath between clenched teeth. 'Don't you talk to me like that! Instead of wasting your time here jawing with me, why don't you ride out after Skann — track him down, keep an eye on him like I'd do?'

'That was always kind of preposterous!'

'Rescued you from the fix you'd gotten yourself into at the damned Maybelline mine though, didn't it?'

'I didn't get into any fix — I was drygulched someplace else and taken there unconscious.'

'Same difference.'

'Curious reasoning! It's much plainer you landed yourself here by horning in at the Miners' Rest. What is it to you exactly if Skann and his boys put about stories concerning Jennie Bennett and Joseph Darcy? About the killing of Ryan Bennett?'

Poverty Joe hissed but made no reply.

'Well . . . ?'

'I refuse to listen or talk.'

'Then if that's the way you feel, I'll set aside conferring with you. Seems, anyway, you're deaf when you don't want to hear and dumb when you don't want to speak. I'll try something else.'

'There is nothing else. Call yourself a detective — a troublebuster? Cord Skann has to be run down and stopped. Isn't there anyone who can do that?'

Joshua was on the edge of telling him to go to hell, but he thought, don't let him rile you.

'I've a hunch there's an easier way to shed some light on the mix-up going on here,' he said.

'Can't be.'

'I'm not so sure. I figure the quickest way to reach conclusions is to wire Miss Flora Bennett. I aim to tell her developments have revealed the only way she can serve her best interests will be to come to Silverville straight away . . . on tomorrow's stage if possible.'

Poverty Joe stiffened. 'I don't think

that's a good idea. Silverville is no place for a city lady.'

'Her sister-in-law has coped all right,' Joshua said drily.

'Mrs Bennett has good and support-ive friends.'

'Yeah, I've seen . . . ' Joshua said without amplifying. 'And I happen to have observed Mrs Bennett is not only charming but reciprocates, accommo-dating one friend mighty generously.'

'What are you trying to say?'

'I figure you might've known, but seeing as how you're not able to answer my questions, maybe it's best I don't answer yours.'

No way, of course, could Joshua describe the goings-on he'd accidentally been witness to from the back yard of the Bennett mansion. But he'd given Poverty Joe something to think about.

His agitation was a small joy to behold. And funny, as in odd. Why would Poverty Joe care if he could persuade Flora Bennett to travel per-sonally to Silverville?

It was a good parting thrust for Joshua, and he did indeed intend to send that wire, better than post-haste. 'For now, I'll get out of your wool and down to the telegraph office,' he told the wounded man.

'It'll be a bad thing to do, Joshua Dillard! You *mustn't*!' Poverty croaked as he made for the stairs.

'You're not making sense, Poverty,' Joshua threw back. 'Lie down and be a good patient for Doctor Pike!'

★   ★   ★

At that moment, Marshal Charley Broadstreet had also gone calling. Joshua Dillard's unexpected entry had precipitated a crisis in the Silverville game. The hand he held would never be stronger and he needed to play his cards. Now.

Jennie Bennett and Joseph Darcy were people of power, yet they also had secrets he'd not been able to uncover but that surely made them vulnerable.

If Dillard kept delving, the little empire in the mountains the pair was building could easily tumble, and with the crash would go his chances of fulfilling his own dreams of a share in a mining town fortune. And more.

Broadstreet's agenda of ambition also had a side to it that no one was aware of except himself. As he hastened to the Bennett mansion, he smiled a sour smile.

Jennie and Darcy thought they were using him — as for a fact they had been. But the time had come for him to claim a bigger reward than he'd so far been allowed.

Jennie Bennett was a beautiful piece of goods. Most everybody in town was agreed on that. Even in her widow's weeds — or maybe because of them — she set eyeballs popping. Smart, too, to the extent that she'd used her charms to enlist the services of her late husband's secretary to preserve and boost her inheritance.

One of Jennie's and Darcy's secrets

was surely open to much of the community. Even a newcomer like Dillard could figure it. The widow was philandering with Darcy. Well, when a woman was willing for stuff like that there could be more than one lucky beggar . . .

A secret no one knew was that he, Broadstreet, lusted after a piece of the same action. Many was the time his insides had squirmed like a worm on a pin when he'd seen unmistakable evidence of the delights Jennie participated in with Darcy. He, too, craved to experience them. Thinking about it kept him awake nights, wondering how much prettier the young widow would look in a dress that wasn't black . . . without a dress at all.

She had the smooth, clear-skinned allure of youth, and it was protected from the sun with a parasol whenever she walked out. Her well-brushed blonde hair gleamed. Her eyes were very blue; her mouth was very red, and very soft . . .

Today was the day Broadstreet had to set about realizing attainment of his goals; to taste the physical reality of the fantasy that simmered within him, firing his blood. He had a suspicion Dillard's mysterious 'business' would otherwise dash his chances. He could also use the threat he figured Dillard somehow posed to Jennie Bennett and her live-in beau to press his advantage.

Today he meant to shift his dealings with the lovely Jennie on to a more intimate level. He thought he knew how to cuckold the man playing illicit consort to the pretty blonde some were calling the Queen of Silverville.

He rang the bell at their imposing front porch. Its summary jangle escalated his tingle of anticipation.

* * *

Jennie Bennett received the marshal in her well-appointed front parlour where she was engaged in perusing some new song sheets that had arrived from

Denver. She did enjoy her singing, though now her favourite piano accompanist was no longer at close call, opportunities for it were not as frequent as she would like.

It was one of the irksome penalties imposed on her life since the flight from the city.

'We'll be comfortable here, thank you, Maria,' she told her maid, wondering what urgency had prompted Charley Broadstreet's visit and regretting that her man was late in returning from a tour of inspection of one of their mines.

The starchy-uniformed Mexican maid who'd shown him in, bobbed her head and left quickly, taught that such was the required routine in this unconventional household. Dismissal was an order to withdraw discreetly and completely. You eaves-dropped or spied on pain of being fired instantly. Much went on within the house's walls that would shock a girl raised as a good Catholic.

Jennie asked, 'Is there a problem, Mr Broadstreet?'

'Prob'ly . . . '

He grinned as he spoke. Like a wolf, Jennie thought. Despite what she'd told the maid, she did not feel comfortable alone with him. But where the law was concerned, and given the singular circumstances of her residency in Silverville, it was wise for any interview to be out of servants' earshot.

Unlike most of the citizenry, Jennie did not hold the marshal in spotless regard, though she was thankful he maintained a town that was relatively orderly for all its raw origins. She sensed Broadstreet had a high opinion of himself and, at bottom, the smart betterment of his own situation was paramount with him.

He was also not her epitome of a gentleman, but Western men often weren't. Though claims were made to the contrary, in Silverville and similar Rocky Mountain communities, men did not deign to moderate behaviour or language. An English lady traveller in the district had recorded that bad temper and profanity in the presence of women was wide-spread. She'd given an example of a stage driver who never spoke without an oath and cursed his splendid teams constantly.

From her own sheltered experience, Jennie knew the report to be true and that Broadstreet exemplified it.

On previous occasions when they'd been in shared company, she'd also caught him casting hungry looks in her direction. She wondered if he knew that these had been noted; if he cared anyway. Though not wishing to indulge in self-flattery, she believed she'd seen a man burning with desire.

'What's the trouble?' she asked briskly. 'It isn't the Skann gang again, is it?'

'Not exactly, though the bastards play a part.'

Another heart-stopping thought leapt into her mind.

'Nothing's happened to *Mr Darcy*,

has it, Marshal?'

'Not as I'm aware, yet . . . And why not call me Charley rather than Marshal? I reckon it's high time we loosened up a little, got more friendly, especially as I figure you're going to need some favours done.'

'Need favours?' she asked, a tremble coming into her voice. 'What on earth are you talking about?'

It crossed her mind that Charley Broadstreet had taken on a confidence and familiarity unwarranted by his station. She was alarmed.

'A detective is in town asking questions,' Broadstreet said.

'I know. A former Pinkerton man. He was here. Mr Darcy and I saw him. It was about the murder in Denver. We couldn't help him. He was sent away. Then he was involved in a fracas with the Skann crowd at the Miners' Rest. Our friend Poverty Joe was injured in the shooting. But didn't you arrest him?'

Broadstreet smirked at her. 'Yeah, but

153

the latest news is I had no grounds to hold him and he hasn't quit town. I figure he aims to stay and do some more digging — and it won't be for silver!'

'Oh, that's impossible!' she gasped in anguish. 'Joe's wounding is bad enough. It mustn't be allowed. What can be done?'

The marshal made a show of pondering, frowning and stroking his jaw.

'I guess I could re-arrest Dillard, trump up some charge, make him wait for the circuit judge. Maybe he could try to break out . . . maybe he'd die while escaping lawful custody. These things happen time to time — '

'I don't want to know!' she cried, clapping her hands to her ears. 'Just let it happen, please!'

Broadstreet grinned again, more broadly.

'Now we're getting somewhere. But it's risky work, organizing a thing like that. Howsoever, you could make it worth my while . . . if the payoff was appropriate and satisfying to a man with powerful fierce needings . . . '

She jerked, her back stiffening.

'I don't like what I think you're suggesting, Marshal!'

'Charley from now on, remember? And I ain't proposing anything that a widow-woman won't have done before — that this widow-woman prob'ly does most every day with her Mr Darcy. There'll be no abusing of innocence or dispelling of ignorance, will there? Think about it.'

She felt her cheeks burning. 'I have, and it's abominable!'

'How so? Is it any different with Darcy?'

'Of course! He's my — he's good to me! Always!'

'Your sweetheart, huh? And for how long has this been? Do you love him?'

'I owe him everything!'

'That doesn't and does answer the question. I eliminate Dillard — get him, and Skann maybe, off your backs, leaving you free — then you'll owe me. Fact, seeing you all hot and spirited minds me to claim a first payment right now!'

Though all the warnings had been there, Broadstreet's lunge caught Jennie by surprise.

11

The Wolf Pounces

She was knocked backwards. The edge of the brocade-covered *chaise-longue* struck her calves and she landed on it, sprawling.

Broadstreet made a strange, wolfish sound and hurled himself on top of her, pinning her with his own heavy body and driving the breath from her lungs. His hands clawed at her clothes as she sank into the yielding upholstery. It was impossible to push up, to escape.

Jennie let loose a squeal like a frightened mouse swooped on by a predatory owl.

'Marshal! *Marshal* — are you mad? *Don't!*'

But her protests were quickly smothered as his mouth sought and found her lips.

For several moments, there was a sound in the Bennett mansion's fine parlour like a noise in the wilderness when a small, captured creature wriggles and kicks in an agony of panic.

She tried to bite him, but he pulled back and backhanded her spitefully across the face.

'Oh, you devil!' she cried.

'Struggling can only make it harder on yourself,' he warned, his voice hard with anger. 'You don't want Darcy to find you bruised and battered to pieces, do you? Perfectly worn out like a two-bit whore at sunrise?'

And it was true. The position was hopeless. Jennie quickly forced herself to stay still and rigid . . . to accept the awful thing that was about to happen to her. It was not compliance, it was resignation.

Panting with excitement, Broadstreet raised on his knees between her spread legs. He held her down with one hand; with the other, he threw up her skirt, exposing her legs and the finest lawn, which he pulled at so hard it ripped.

'I didn't realize you looked so good!'

Red marks glowed dully on white flesh where he'd manhandled her, but careless of her hurts, he pressed on, completion of his pleasure the sole consideration.

And then, from outside the room, but within the house, came interruption in the sound of hurried approach. The footfalls reached the closed door.

'Jennie?'

'Darcy . . . ' Broadstreet muttered between clenched teeth. He clapped a hand over her mouth. 'Stay quiet!'

But the caution was too late.

The door opened. An angry cry boomed out.

'What's going on here?'

Jennie sobbed, 'He attacked me! He took me by force — '

Another roar came from the doorway, then chaos broke loose.

While Jennie writhed on her back in the tangle of her disarranged clothing, Broadstreet rolled off her. He hit the floor with his shoulder, rolled and rose to one knee. He hadn't got around to removing the single gun-belt he wore high on the left-hand side, butt angled to the right. He grabbed for it in a cross-draw.

'Now wait a minute, Darcy!' he rapped. 'Don't do anything rash! I've got the measure of you two love-birds — '

It was not enough to quell the rage of a man who saw his loved one violated.

Shock registered on Broadstreet's face as he saw a double-barrelled pistol brought from a shoulder holster and levelled first. Frantically, he triggered, but the other gun boomed a split second ahead of his own. A heavy, steel-jacketed bullet pierced his belly and hurled him back against a tall dresser, doubling him up. His own shot thudded ineffectively into rich carpet an inch from his adversary's boot cap.

Broadstreet slid, legs collapsing beneath him. China on the rocking dresser's shelves rattled but didn't fall.

Darcy watched him crumple, the smoking muzzle of the derringer clenched in his fist following him all the way down. But no second, finishing shot was necessary.

The marshal was dead with staring eyes that saw nothing more.

On the *chaise-longue*, Jennie felt solicitous hands and arms reach for her, trying to cradle her. But she curled into a ball of shame and fear.

'He was a lawman. He threatened me — us! — with exposure,' she began to explain. 'I think he *knew*. Oh, God, I thought he was our friend; that he would protect us from the awful Cord Skann!'

The man who shared her life gazed fixedly into her tear-stained face. 'So did I. I never suspected — '

'When will we be safe? Another killing! Why is the man dead?'

The reply was full of suppressed fury.

'Don't lose your head, my dear! Broadstreet is dead because he's proved himself nothing more than a dirty blackmailer and rapist — a disgrace to his badge! I fear he got what was coming to him.'

'Oh, it's a nightmare! We've done enough running already,' she whimpered.

He nodded grimly. 'And we'll do no more! I'm sorry this has had to happen to you, Jennie. But we mustn't let the swine's foulness destroy our dreams. His death can't weigh on our consciences. We've survived worse blows. We'll work through this, too. There'll be a way . . . '

* * *

Joshua Dillard waited in frustration in the Silverville stage station. It was the day after he'd sent his urgent wire to Flora Bennett and received a testy reply with her reluctant agreement to ride a stage ticket to the primitive mining town.

Now the coach was running behind time and he knew in his bones that its lateness would irritate his arriving client still further. He got up from the hard wooden bench and paced about waiting room cum booking office. But the place was dingy and cramped. The clerk behind the desk scowled as the toes of Joshua's knee-high boots collided with express packages and luggage dumped about on the gritty floor in seemingly disorderly heaps.

'Where is this stage?' Joshua asked.

The clerk didn't get to answer because his attention was taken by the arrival of a new customer, lugging a bulging carpet bag and, in a heavy cape, plainly dressed for travel.

'Maria Santo!' he exclaimed. 'Where the hell d'you think you'd be goin'?'

'I must quit town, Senor Jack. For good. I return to my family in El Paso and go to Denver to board the train.'

The clerk looked doubtful. 'Railroad fare ain't cheap. You sure you got the dinero?'

'*Sí*, plenty dinero, but it is not anyone's business! I must not talk with you — no gossip, Mrs Bennett say. Just sell me the stagecoach ride, *por favor*.'

Maria opened a reticule. Joshua couldn't help but see it was bulging with rolled and banded greenbacks.

'Mrs Bennett and Mr Darcy happy 'bout your goin' home?' the clerk asked.

'It is Mr Darcy who pay.'

The clerk was puzzled and frowned. 'Very kind of him, I'm sure.'

Insistence shone in the Mexican girl's eyes. 'Enough, Señor Jack, no? I must have this ticket without delay, else Mr Darcy and Mrs Bennett, they *muy enojado*.'

'Señor Jack' shrugged, sold her the ticket and the exchange ended with Maria plumping herself down on the bench alongside other waiting passengers.

Some small domestic crisis for the Bennett household, Joshua noted. The distraction over, his thoughts returned to his own problems.

What was holding up the damned stage from Denver?

* ★ ★

Though Joshua didn't know it, the main problem was that the stage, already running behind schedule, was literally being held up.

The coach was a battered Concord that lurched and bounced upon its leather thoroughbraces along a road that was all ruts and stones and holes. Alpine slopes rose and fell around it, sometimes dizzyingly sheer, the rock multi-coloured, red and ochre and weather-stained. And desolate. No life showed except for splotches of brush and, here and there, the stunted pine or cedar, spared the lumberjack's axe, that cast a pathetic shadow in cold, clear sunlight.

The coach had a driver, no guard and four passengers, one of whom was a very peeved Flora Bennett. It was really too bad that she was paying a detective recommended for independence of action but who was summoning her to an odious and godforsaken mining camp in the mountains. She'd hired Dillard partly with an eye to avoiding such a tedious excursion.

'*Your presence is absolutely vital to your interests and a swift conclusion to the case . . .*'

Only because she considered the ex-Pinkerton a savvy, hard-headed man, not prone to exaggeration, was she paying attention to his request.

She'd also hired him because he was said to get results, but was perpetually short of money and thus not overly expensive. She'd guarded against a loss on the deal by linking his payment to the results he achieved. But she remembered — with an inward flinch of embarrassment now — that she'd also promised him something more than money to whet his appetite for the unpromising assignment.

If he really was about to deliver the inheritance her lost brother had intended her to have, she would have to make good on her promise. For she was a woman of her word.

This was a slightly scary prospect, but in all frankness she had to admit it did excite her as well. She was not the insensitive and frigid spinster of her reputation. She found Joshua Dillard ruggedly handsome and — well, an interesting person. Much more so than the gentlemen who pestered her for her company in the grand reception rooms and churches and opera houses of Denver where the wealthy and their offspring mingled and frolicked.

And in the West, the attitude to liaisons not sanctified by marriage was a tolerant 'live and let live'. The women who ran the parlour houses in Denver, for example, were very intelligent in the running of their businesses. Their activities were open and they had circles of admiring and influential friends.

While she daydreamed, wheels whirred on axles, timber and leather creaked, and six horses' hoof-beats made a monotonous clop on the hard roadway.

Presently, the teams' gait began to lag

and the driver hauled them up in a dip where the road forded a small stream and was shaded by one of the few substantial stands of timber.

He kicked on the brake, put his whip in the bracket and, leaning over, yelled down to his passengers.

'Breather fer the hosses! Yuh c'n step out an' stretch your legs if'n it pleases yuh.'

Flora was helped down by one of the two male passengers. It was an awkward stopping-place, chosen more for the benefit of the stage-line's horses than its passengers. As they stumbled clear of the coach, stiff and aching, the other woman — the plump, middle-aged wife of the other man — looked up and emitted a startled shriek.

'A bandit!'

A horseman had ridden out from between the trees' thick boles, pointing a shotgun. He wore a hat with its brim pulled well down and yelled orders muffled by the red cloth pulled up over his face.

'Stay still, everyone! Grab for the sky, and don't any of you make a move!'

For Flora Bennett, turning and finding herself looking into the muzzle of a loaded and pointed shotgun was a novel and frightening experience.

To make clear he meant business, the gunman cocked the right hammer of the weapon with an ominous click. Then he let go the barrel's load into a patch of thorny brush.

Pellets and bits of vegetation seemed to fly in all directions but no one was hit. On the heels of the blast's roar, the plump woman's scream mingled with the echo.

Still on his high seat, the driver groaned.

'Aw, hell, mister! Yuh've made a mistake an' picked the wrong coach. Ain't no money aboard — not even a strongbox, an' that's gospel! Jest some ol' letters is all — '

'Quit blathering, Jehu! There's only one thing I want from you — you leave behind that fine lady passenger with the plumed hat who last stepped down from the coach. The rest of you, beat it out of here! Understand?'

The demand produced a concerted murmur of shock and indignation.

'Why,' the driver said, 'that's kidnappin', 'cept she'd be a grown lady! Call it abduction, white-slavin' or some-such . . . is thar a ransom demand?'

'No ransom,' the bandit growled through his mask.

'You plumb loco then?'

The bandit lifted his shotgun higher.

'You've too much lip, mister. Shuddup, or you'll collect a bellyful of buckshot! Remember, I've a second barrel left. The rest of you people, get aboard! The coach is going.'

Another metallic noise came from the shotgun.

Appreciating he was set up on the box like a clay pigeon, the driver rapidly changed his mind about pursuing the debate.

'Christ, man, don't go to shootin' ag'in with thet scattergun!'

'Get your rig moving then! I've a whole pocketful of buckshot shells. I'm tired and hurting, my finger's getting awful itchy, and I've little patience for argumentative old fools!'

The driver's leathery face turned a shade of dirty white. Without ado, he had the brake kicked off and was shaking out the lines, yelling and flourishing the whip. The frightened horses jumped into action. The coach rocked as hoofs and wheels splashing through the shallow waters of the ford, sending up spray that twinkled like silver in the sunlight.

'Now that's better . . . ' the hold-up artist said.

Left alone with him in the mountain wilderness, Flora Bennett felt very afraid. She tried not to stare at him. The coach was diminishing rapidly to a dot and a muffled rumble in the distance.

'I swear to God I have nothing you would want,' she said as evenly as her quivering would allow. 'You must have had the wrong coach and you surely have the wrong person.'

He chuckled, but there was no humour in it.

'I don't think so, ma'am.'

'You'll be sorry when this is reported and a posse is sent and arrests you!'

But she didn't think that was likely to happen.

12

Missing Persons

By setting out for Silverville, she'd fallen into a trap!

What did this road agent intend? Was she to be murdered — silenced by commission of the parties she believed had cheated her of her share of her brother's fortune?

Strangely, she was possessed of a sudden intuition that the bandit was someone she knew, or had at least met before. But how? The feeling was utterly unreasonable. She didn't associate with ruffians or desperadoes.

She wondered if Joshua Dillard was a party to the growing conspiracy she suspected. But he, too, might have been duped. What if he was already dead and the wire message and summons had been a fake sent under his name?

Gripped by the horror of her predicament, but with spots of angry colour on her cheeks, Flora waited for her captor's next move.

'I've got a mule waiting behind the trees,' he said. 'Even brought a side-saddle. You see, I'm civilized — I don't expect a lady to ride astride. We're going to my place, *Miss Bennett*. You and I have a lot to talk about.'

He knew her name! She could definitely no longer fool herself he'd made a mistake in picking her out from the other stage passengers.

★ ★ ★

Outside the stage station in Silverville, the air filled with a buzz of anticipation. Word quickly spread: the stage from Denver was coming. Its dust banner had been spotted entering the eastern end of the valley at a fast lick.

Joshua had grown tired of killing time in the cramped waiting-room. He'd moved his bruised body and still mildly

174

aching head to a neighbouring café. It was a seedy place where he ate an indifferent serving of steak, potatoes and eggs slowly, asking for a second cup of coffee, though he could ill-afford to spend his dangerously shrunken expenses coin. Damn, wasn't it always the way? Soon as he had some cash in hand, even if he spent it promptly and wisely, the advantage was somehow whipped away.

The coffee was a black and bitter brew, but it did seem to lift his drowsiness. He perked up some more when the loafers on the street began to head for the stage-line office and corrals.

He went out.

The coach came storming into the township at a breakneck pace, slewed as the brake was put on, then straightened out. The horses, reined in and recognizing the run's end, blew through wide nostrils and shook slobber from their chins. The late stage from Denver came to a jolting halt in a dust cloud of its own making.

The driver spilled from the box like his pants were afire.

'A hold-up, by God! We was held up!'

Joshua gaped, but then quickly started across at a jog.

The crowd surrounded the sweaty, dust-streaked driver and began firing a fusillade of questions.

'Shut up!' Joshua yelled. 'Let him be heard!'

He had a sick premonition about what was going to be revealed.

The driver eagerly told his would-be interrogators, 'The robber didn't take no cash — no freight, no mails. He stole a lady passenger — kidnapped her yuh might say, the dirty sonofabitch!'

A hubbub of scandalized speculation arose from the audience hanging on his words. For Joshua, it was different. The details of the hold-up sent a cold rage stealing over him. He swore.

The ruffled passengers were emerging from the Concord. Two men, one middle-aged woman. No cool and composed — or even hot and angry

— Flora Bennett. It was exactly as he'd worst feared as soon as he'd heard the driver's astonishing report.

'Who was this gent with the gun?' Joshua asked the driver.

'Dunno . . . he was masked with a red bandanna.'

'How did it happen?'

'We'd stopped at the ford to let the horses blow an' the ladies an' gents to — uh — stretch their legs, like always. He rode out from the trees with a goddamned shotgun and let go a load of buckshot. It was sure scary.'

Someone broke in, 'The damned maniac's gotta be tracked down! The stage company has a responsibility!'

'Fetch Marshal Broadstreet!' the driver croaked. He hadn't liked the sound of the word responsibility and he meant to capitalize on his celebrity while he could. 'Bring a man who was bare inches from death a strong drink!'

The deputy who'd accompanied Charley Broadstreet at the Miners' Rest shouldered his way forward.

'The drink's no problem, driver, but I can't promise the marshal. Broadstreet ain't been seen since late yesterday. Must've ridden out on some job without telling anyone.'

An arthritic hostler who'd limped over from the livery stables said, 'But his hoss is still in its stall.'

'Mebbe taken another then,' the deputy grumbled. 'Anyhow, the marshal ain't on call, and I got the town to handle on my own.'

Listening to this, Joshua cussed again, savagely.

'Are you telling us Marshal Broadstreet has gone missing?'

'I ain't saying he has and I ain't saying he ain't. But what's it to you, mister? Weren't you told to attend to your business and mosey on?'

Joshua ignored the question. 'That makes two missing persons!' he exclaimed harshly. Almost to himself, he added in a mutter, 'Three if you count Zach Skann . . .'

Lips bloodless, he tried putting more

questions to both the stage driver and the deputy lawman. He quickly learned that they knew nothing more than the bald facts that two people had vanished in strange circumstances in or around Silverville. He figured his own actions had triggered one if not both disappearances.

He'd put his client in harm's way and he was unable to rely on the official law to help him recover her since its representative coincidentally — or maybe not coincidentally — had departed, or been removed from, the scene.

Hell, wasn't this always his luck? Another job that was going to bring him no profit and maybe a whole heap of trouble. If he could say it was 'no nevermind' that evil parties were making a fool of him, now would be the time to saddle up, cut and run before he found himself the subject of awkward questions or hostile intervention from those responsible for the Rye Bennett murder and the evasions that had followed it.

But quitting a case didn't sit comfortably with Joshua Dillard. It was something he just didn't do. Come hell or high water, he'd carried the fight to lawbreakers unremittingly since the death of his wife in San Antonio. He'd resigned from the Pinkerton Agency because it had frowned on his obsessive passion for moral justice and his dubious, reckless methods. Years had passed but his resolve, his hatred of those prepared to kill the innocent for whatever reason, be it vengeance, profit or sheer bloody-mindedness, was as strong as ever.

So what was his next move?

Questions in Silverville were going to produce no quick answers. Did he ride to the ford and try to pick up whatever tracks had been left by Flora Bennett and her mysterious abductor?

That, too, would be a laborious matter and, though he did pride himself on his skills as a tracker in wild country, an outcome was never certain, especially when the terrain was also hard and mountainous.

It was then Joshua remembered Poverty Joe and the questionable stance he had taken over his self-confessed friends, Joseph Darcy and Jennie Bennett.

Now more than ever it was imperative that Poverty should be made to speak out. He had to tell what he knew, and to reveal his true involvement in the fight against the Skann bunch. At least one life — Flora Bennett's — could hang on it. Would he still be mule-headed stubborn?

The stage driver and the excited crowd were adjourning to a saloon were the driver was committed to repeating his harrowing tale for what surely amounted to entertainment. Joshua headed urgently for Dr Ambrose Pike's hospital.

The door of the house opened to his push and the bell pealed within. This time, Joshua didn't wait. He took the stairs two at a time and made for the room where he'd last spoken to Poverty Joe.

Pike appeared in the passage before him, gaunt and gnome-like.

'Sir — !'

But Joshua rudely strode past him, contemptuous of his protest and the restraining, long-fingered hand he tried to lay on his arm.

'Mr Dillard, you're wasting your time! The patient you presumably wish to see has gone. Didn't you know?'

Joshua swung. 'Gone! What do you mean?'

The little doctor did some stiff raging of his own.

'The crazy fool discharged himself sometime in the night! I can't protect patients from their stupidity, can I?'

A gasp, a gape, then Joshua continued through the door to the room where he'd confidently expected to find Poverty Joe, propped up against pillows, letting a bullet wound heal and his body replace lost blood.

Though he'd been warned, he gaped again. It was getting to be a habit.

It was true. Poverty wasn't there; not

any more. Injured or not, he'd either spirited himself away or been taken away by parties unknown.

He thought the first explanation, which was the one Doc Pike offered, was the most likely. He'd over-estimated the effects of Poverty's injuries or under-estimated his determination.

The result was the same: another missing person.

'The man's conduct really is deplorable,' Doc Pike complained.

He left him to regret the loss of his patient. He supposed the medico's consternation had more to do with hurt professional pride than expense. Unlike Joshua, he was having his bill in the matter paid ... because the odd hermit had Jennie Bennett and Joshua Darcy, no less, to come to his aid.

How had the pair become his friends and benefactors? That was another question Poverty Joe had never answered. Joshua was more determined than ever that he should.

After giving the mounting problems

some thought, he decided that if Poverty Joe had left Doc Pike's under his own steam, the likeliest place he'd find him would be the old, isolated cabin that was his out-of-town home.

Finding that neither Poverty's horse nor mule were at the livery stables tended to confirm his guess. Joshua was considerably tired of being thwarted. Spending yet more of his dwindling expenses money from Flora Bennett, he hired a nag.

But this decision, and acting on it, came too late to prevent another unwelcome twist; another fresh disaster.

★ ★ ★

Shock had followed shock for Flora Bennett after she was removed from the Denver-Silverville stage. The first was her discovery of the identity of her abductor, whom she recognized the instant she saw him without the mask of the red bandanna.

He had brought her to a lonely but

solid cabin, old but lately patched, at the end of a dim trail that ended high on a ridge, among whispering pines. It was a right nice place he had here, quiet and simple, fitted out for an educated gentleman's comfort with a proper floor, furniture and shelves of books.

At first she was coldly furious, then considerable explaining was done. But it brought her only the briefest spell of relief.

The raiders came without warning, whooping and yelling like savages, though they were plainly white men.

'Joe!' she screamed. 'Who are they?'

'Cord Skann and his pals!' he said. 'He's gotten wise to my spying and meddling. I fear I've made a godawful mistake bringing you here. He means to force a showdown! Can you handle a gun?'

'A gun? No — of course not!'

'Then it's going to be the worst for us. They'll sack this place — maybe kill us both. Skann has vowed to destroy everything and punish everyone connected with the Bennett interests. Now I've spoken out — declared my colours in the Miners' Rest — I'm an easy target. What a fool I've been! Out here, away from town with no law in calling distance, a man has to fight on his lonesome!'

'What about a woman?'

He was reluctant to tell her. 'They'll not go easy on you, specially if they learn who you are. Just being here with me will give them excuse to pick on you; treat you rough.'

'What does that mean?'

He told her no reassuring lies.

'I regret that once our defences are broken these skunks will figure they can enjoy an attractive woman however it pleases them.'

Flora shuddered, her face drained white. Her position was going in leaps and bounds from bad to worse.

Outside, a big man with straggly hair and a prominent nose hauled up his horse and called out.

'I want you to face me, Poverty Joe! I know you're in thar, an' I'm callin' you out!'

'Go to hell, Cord Skann!' Poverty said. 'You and your boys are outlaws. There's no one here to see fair play. Show myself and you'll fill me with holes! Besides, I'm no gunfighter.'

Flora saw that the attackers were dismounting in the cover of the trees and moving in on the cabin on foot, crouching behind the thickest boles.

Cord Skann said, 'Suit yourself. We brought plenty of shells. You ain't got a dewdrop's chance in hell of gettin' clear anyways.'

To underline that he was making no idle boast, he gave his gunhawks a nod. It produced a rattle of gunfire and a storm of lead that thunked into the cabin's walls and shattered a window.

'Go through to the lean-to,' Poverty ordered Flora. 'Get down behind the woodpile there and don't come out for anything.'

'Joe, this is crazy — '

'Don't argue — just do it!'

Poverty tried to slam a shutter across the broken window, but more lead chopped through it and he was forced to huddle beneath it, trusting to the thickness of the wall for protection.

Flora abandoned her protest and made a wild scuttle for the rear door and the flimsier, brush-thatched lean-to where the horse and mule were tethered.

She didn't think the woodpile offered a particularly secure hiding-place, yet hid there because she saw nothing better. She was no feeble, wilting flower of a woman, but knew the thick of a gun battle was no place for her. It was something quite outside her experience.

She was also sure that her lone protector's goose was cooked.

Out front, Cord Skann yelled, 'I'm gonna kill you, Poverty Joe! Then you'll disappear — just like I reckon your friends made my brother disappear!'

More shots rang out, some of them

from within the cabin. The man they'd called Poverty Joe was shooting back. But Flora had seen he was heavily outnumbered and her doubts for her safety grew.

13

Shock After Shock

Joshua Dillard, riding the most direct trail to the cabin on the ridge lickety-spit, saw ahead of him a buckboard. A man and woman were on its seat. As he drew closer, he was surprised to recognize the couple as Jennie Bennett and Joseph Darcy. Somehow he'd expected them to be using a less utilitarian conveyance: a smart buggy drawn by a handsome span of glistening blacks maybe.

But when he caught up with them he noticed that they had a tarpaulin-wrapped bundle loaded in the tray.

'Howdy!' he greeted them. 'Branching into freight?'

Darcy frowned and didn't respond in kind to his intended banter.

'No, we're riding out to inspect the

old Maybelline mine,' he said quickly. 'We understand Cord Skann, who was squatting there, decamped after the gunfight you had in the Miners' Rest.'

Jennie Bennett forced a sweet smile. 'We own the mine, you see.'

Joshua laughed. 'Along with many others!'

'But not all abandoned, fortunately! Don't let us delay you, Mr Dillard. And thank you for ridding the place of Cord Skann.'

Joshua touched the brim of his hat. 'A pleasure, ma'am . . . Mr Darcy. I hope you're right about Skann.'

Darcy said, 'We'll take our chances.'

'Well, be careful.'

Joshua passed them and urged his rented mount back into a gallop. He'd made no mention that their friend Poverty Joe had quit his paid-for bed at Doc Pike's . . . and, he was beginning to suspect, might be the lone bandit who'd held up the stage from Denver and carried off Flora Bennett!

Not many moments later, almost lost

in the drumming of his horse's hoofbeats, he thought he heard a faint crackle of distant gunfire way up ahead.

He kept the horse moving at a run.

His alarm deepened when he saw a plume of black smoke rising into the sky like a smudge of charcoal dirtying the blue. It came from behind the trees that hid Poverty Joe's cabin.

★   ★   ★

They found Flora after the shooting had stopped and they were getting ready to fire the place, splashing lamp oil through the main structure.

Flora feared the only man who might have saved her from the outlaws must be dead, or dying. She was emerging from behind the woodpile to make a dash for a possibly safer hiding place among the pines when one of the raiders came through into the lean-to from the cabin.

She ducked back, but it was too late. He'd seen her.

'Hey, lookee what I've found — a woman! Seems Poverty Joe was a slyer dog than we thought.'

He was about forty, square-headed and broad in the shoulders and arms. Mean-eyed.

Her heart raced. She was not only discovered but cornered.

'Fancy lady, ain't she?' the finder said. 'Smells nice, ain't fat, ain't thin.'

She said, 'How dare you talk so disrespectfully! Get away from me, you — you savages!'

Other men were crowding in behind the first. 'Hoity-toity,' one commented.

'No matter,' said the mean-eyed man. 'She's fetchin' in all the important points. She'll serve good as any easy saloon gal. Better, I'll bet!'

'She ain't willin', Flip.'

Flip grinned and winked. 'So? If'n she chooses to fight, ain't we more'n one, don't pards do an' share alike?'

'We ain't got time fer foolin' with a female, Flip, an' we don't want no prisoners. Cord says we gotta pull out

193

fast now an' fort up at the Maybelline. Thar's no knowing what Charley Broadstreet has in mind. Nor the Dillard feller.'

Flip spurned the warning with a sneer.

'Aw, quit fussin', Bud. Back at the mine, we all been wantin' fierce fer five minutes' fun. This ain't gonna make no diff'rence . . . '

Nobody needed to draw Flora any picture. The notion that all western men were gentlemen was an absurd fallacy promulgated by land developers and other investors. The experiences of many women who travelled to the frontier gave the lie to it. She knew that for her the five minutes wouldn't be fun but hell. And they would make a huge and horrifying difference.

Flip pushed her back on top of the woodpile and seized and lifted her ankles. She tried to kick, but it only uncovered more of her neat, calfskin half-boots, which he grabbed and tugged.

'Let's git these off fer a start!'
She shrieked.
The stabled mule brayed.
The men laughed.

* * *

Joshua thought: *Poverty Joe!* He remembered the gunfire he'd heard, and now it seemed the cabin high on the ridge, among the trees, must be on fire. Nothing else in that direction could produce such a quantity of black smoke.

Had Poverty Joe taken Flora Bennett off the stage? He recalled how set Poverty had been against him bringing his client to Silverville when he'd announced the intention at Doc Pike's. It struck him as very possible.

The other question he asked himself was, if the first conjecture was right, what effect did the latest shooting and evident arson have on Flora? The consequences could be disastrous to his own position.

He could understand why Cord

Skann and his gang would have scores to settle with Poverty Joe. He was a friend of Jennie Bennett and Joseph Darcy and had precipitated the fracas at the Miners' Rest.

What would the evil gang have done with Flora Bennett? Would Cord Skann recognize her as the sister of the man his brother had hated?

He rode like the wind to reach the piney ridge. It took less than five minutes. The moment he rounded the trees, the sight of the burning cabin filled his eyes and the smoke's acrid reek his nostrils.

Single-handed, no one could do anything to save the place. That would take a bucket chain and a generous supply of water. Then he saw the two people he was looking for.

Flora Bennett was dragging Poverty Joe to safety from the fiery scene. He reined in, jumped down and rushed to help her.

Though she'd presented herself to him before as nothing less than immaculate, she was ragged and filthy. Her hands were black from beating her way out of the fire and blood was spreading on to her ripped dress from her limp burden.

She said only, 'Mr Dillard — !' before she collapsed in a sprawl.

Joshua turned his attention first to Poverty Joe. He had suffered a fresh bullet wound but was still alive, though barely conscious. He was shot high in the chest and blood was soaking his vest, which Joshua tore away.

Flora lifted up, resting her weight on one arm. Despite her soot-smudged face, loose hair and torn dress, she looked lovelier than ever, with a long smooth curve to her body.

In that moment, he also realized that, irrespective of her high-falutin manner and seeming self-centredness, she was a very brave woman.

'What happened?' Joshua said, sticking to the plain and simple.

She brushed the hair from her face with a dirty hand and cried angrily,

'Can't you see? They outnumbered him. He was shot. And four of the cowards who did it fell upon me! They carried on, one after the other, till a man called Cord said they could waste no more time — the shooting might have been heard and they'd be caught. They had to burn down the cabin and ride pronto for the Maybelline . . . whatever that might be.'

Her report made Joshua seethe, but he didn't try to explain the Maybelline was where the bunch had their camp. Silently and bitterly, he cursed himself for the series of disasters he'd failed to anticipate. His client had been assaulted and a man's life left in the balance.

'We need clean cloth — anything to pad the wound, stem the blood loss,' he said in a strained voice. 'Later, the slug will have to be dug out. He was already in poor shape and should have stayed where he was, at the doc's. Poor Poverty Joe!'

Flora threw him a sharp, frowning look.

'No! Not Poverty Joe — why did he choose such a silly name?'

She took off her already torn petticoat and dropped to her knees beside the men — the wounded and the anxious — ripping it into strips.

'Not Poverty Joe,' she said again. 'This is my brother's former secretary, Joseph Darcy.'

Behind them, the roof of the cabin fell in with a crash. Sparks flew and the flames roared voraciously as they licked into the fresh fuel.

14

Turn of the Wheel

In the shade of the pines, as the cabin fire burned itself out, they made Poverty Joe as comfortable as they could. Joshua knew he would have to ride to Silverville to fetch help. But first there were questions which required urgent answers.

Flora Bennett supplied them succinctly, not dwelling on her own hurts.

'Yes, your Poverty Joe is Joseph Darcy,' she said.

Joshua's mind struggled to grasp the import.

'Then who is the man living with Jennie Bennett in Silverville?'

'My brother, Mr Dillard. Rye is alive and trying to build a new life for himself, free from the shadow of his Pinkerton years! Joe Darcy told me all of this after he'd taken me from the stage and brought me to his cabin. It's hard to understand, isn't it? I was shocked myself. But for a few precious moments it was a blessing and a relief, too ... Then Joe told me about the threat posed by Zach Skann's brother, which almost instantly was made cruel reality.'

His mind as close as it could get to boggling, Joshua digested the revelations.

'And you knew none of this?'

Flora shook her head. 'Nothing, I swear. I was broken, sick at heart when I came to Denver for Ryan's funeral. Later, it seemed incredible that his will could have been mislaid and that I should be forgotten, frozen out by Jennie and the supposed Joseph Darcy. Can you imagine how I felt? But Joe told me Rye wanted it this way, so I would be safe from the same enemies who'd pursued and tried to destroy him.'

'When Zach Skann broke into Rye's

house in Denver, Rye and Joe managed to turn the tables on him. In the struggle, he was blown to faceless oblivion with his own shotgun. So the three of them — Rye, Joseph and Jennie — made it look like Zach Skann had been successful and it was Rye who'd been murdered. But it was Rye, wearing Zach's clothes who was seen leaving Capitol Hill in the rain. And it was Zach's virtually headless body that was buried in Rye's clothes in Riverside Cemetery — doused in cheap pomade to hide its smelliness!'

Joshua wondered at it all, but he was beginning to comprehend.

'Of course! The masquerade would have been impossible to maintain in Denver, which explains the shift of Bennett operations to Silverville and the avoidance of Denver friends and associates. But why the masquerade in the first place?'

'Rye didn't want to have to defend himself against a possible charge of slaughtering Skann. He and Jennie also wanted to be free from the multiple threats and fears that had dogged their successful life as a result of his time spent in the Pinkertons. The death of Skann gave them an unprecedented chance that surely would never be repeated. Once Ryan Bennett was gone, the criminal world would no longer hound him, his wife or his businesses.'

'But the plan unravelled.'

Flora nodded. 'They bargained without Skann's vengeful brother, Cord, who rightly figured they'd had a hand in his brother's disappearance. But Cord didn't have enough familiarity with Rye or his secretary to hit on the true explanation. The switch of identities was a perfect cover-up. The real Joseph Darcy is an unassuming man, who has always preferred working behind the scenes. His early 'retirement' in no wise displeased him. He could have his books and his malt whiskey and occasionally could visit and chat with his old employer.'

Joshua kicked himself. Although he'd

known hocus-pocus was in train, and that it involved Poverty Joe, he should have figured out the details for himself. He remembered how Flora had told him that Rye's favourite line was 'always expect the unexpected'. The false 'Joseph Darcy' — Rye Bennett — had used it when speaking to him and Marshal Broadstreet had mentioned he'd been fond of delivering it to him.

And that was only one of the giveaways. There were the surprisingly intimate relations Jennie enjoyed with her 'secretary' and the piano that Poverty Joe — the real Joseph Darcy — liked to play. On reflection, he'd no doubt dredge up further small clues he'd overlooked . . . like how a grizzly old porcupine of a mountain hermit could have become a drinking companion and confidant of the bogus Darcy, a generally unsociable townsman.

Ruefully, he amassed his self-recriminations and recognized that Flora Bennett's legacy, and the lion's share of the promised payment for his efforts, the percentage-based commission, would not be forth-coming. Still, he was not the worst off. He contemplated the chances of the pale, wounded man whose bleeding they'd at last managed to staunch.

He said, 'I guess the real Joe Darcy is the one who has suffered most in — ' He broke off as an alarming thought struck him.

'Did you say Cord Skann and his hell-bent thugs headed out for the Maybelline?'

Flora looked at him inquiringly. 'I did.'

'Goddamnit! I met your brother and his wife while I was riding here. They were going to the Maybelline mine, they said. Thought Skann had quit it. When Skann runs up against them, out of town and without the protection of Marshal Broadstreet, he'll figure his lambs, like Joe, have also come to the slaughter!'

★　★　★

Joshua left Flora with advice to keep Poverty Joe warm and still. If he came round, and it seemed possible for him to move without huge discomfort, they might use Joe's horse and pack mule to make for Silverville.

Joshua's new priority was to warn Ryan and Jennie Bennett that Cord Skann was on the vengeance trail, his blood up. It was all that was left to him if he wanted to salvage anything remotely satisfactory from the sorry adventure.

Why the hell had the couple taken it into their heads to visit an isolated, abandoned mine?

While Joshua rode, he turned over in his mind the verbal bombshells delivered by Flora Bennett, trying to make full sense of them. He rode rapidly, keeping the sturdy rented gelding to a mile-eating gait. Fortunately, the horse seemed accustomed to running continuously at an altitude of 9,000 feet, which would be difficult for the beast or man not used to the high country.

The land made for rugged riding, being much broken, gashed by ravines and spined by stony ridges.

Despite his breakneck pace, he noted signs here and there of the recent passage of a body of riders on the same trail . . . Cord Skann and his nightmare crew at a fair guess. But he caught up with and met no one on the trail.

The day was drawing to a close, the sun in a flushed western sky over snow-tipped Rocky Mountain peaks, when the Maybelline No. 1's decaying structures came into sight. He reined in the gelding and approached cautiously, concealing his mount behind the huge, artificial hill of weed-grown mine tailings. He then climbed and studied the various buildings from a commanding viewpoint.

The Skann bunch's tired horses were hitched alongside the old offices where they'd previously made camp. Another notable indication of occupation was the Bennetts' buckboard standing outside a barn-like erection. But the man he now knew to be Ryan Bennett and his wife, Jennie, were not to be seen. Nor were Skann and his men.

Also missing was the bundle Joshua had seen in the buckboard's tray.

Maybe they were all inside the building which Joshua assumed housed a stamp mill for the crushing of ore. A diverted mountain stream still gushed through the paddles of a giant, motionless water-wheel fixed to its outside, splintered with weather and disuse.

In the mine's working day, the wheel would have driven a horizontal shaft inside the barn. As the shaft rotated, attached cams would have lifted and dropped a battery of heavy steel stamps held vertically, generally in sets of five, in a frame of iron or very solid timber. While the waterwheel was turning, the action would have repeated itself, over and over, with the weighty stamps falling relentlessly by gravity to break and crush the ore fed beneath them.

At that moment, a rear door to the

stamp mill shed opened and two of Skann's followers came out, hefting long-handled, pointed spades.

'The mechanism inside looked fine,' the first said. 'It must be a blockage in the water channel. Weed or somesuch.'

'Some of us git stuck with doin' all the shit work!' the other said. 'We didn't have us a turn of the fun with Poverty Joe's bitch either.'

His companion growled hungrily as though anticipating a tasty meal. 'Mebbe our chance will come with the Jennie Bennett woman! It's gonna be quite a party an' this time I want a piece afore Cord blows his whistle!'

A cold feeling crept over Joshua as their bawdy talk confirmed his fears that the Bennetts had ridden into deep trouble.

The pair got to work around the submerged part of the waterwheel.

'It's damned coontail sure enough, Huck. Pesky, dense stuff.'

After some concerted hacking, they tossed out branches of dark, olive-green weed. The tips were bunched with stiff, whorled leaves, much forked and with small teeth.

Satisfied with the results, they jumped clear and called out. A muffled reply came from inside the shed. With a grating sound, a hidden brake restraining the wheel was released. It began to churn in the powerful stream, at first with a slow rumble, then more freely and faster.

The first man sniggered. 'Now Cord Skann is goin' to have hisself some real excitement! He was fair twitchin' at the notion of givin' 'em their needin's usin' the stamp mill.'

'Long as he don't crush the woman afore we've done some crushing ourselfs . . . '

The two men headed back inside.

Joshua trembled with anger at the horror of what he'd heard. He dragged in a deep, steadying breath.

God, no — no, he thought. Not that!

The stamp mill's cogs must have been engaged to the waterwheel's drive inside the shed. For a pounding began that shook the rocky ground under the entire mining site with rhythmic thumps. The standing buckboard's horses shuffled and whinnied nervously.

Joshua threw aside his remaining caution. He ran and slithered down the steep, unstable slope of the tailings. But no one in the shed heard his precipitous approach above the impact of the stamps on the solid, steel-plated foundation of the ore pit beneath them.

Closing in, he heard voices raised above the din of the ore-crusher. Then the machinery was switched off at an assumed throw of a lever, and the noisy stamps came to a clanking halt. Joshua flattened himself against the shed's warped siding and moved along it to the main doors.

The disconnected waterwheel continued to rotate in the stream on the side of the big shed to the far side of the doors, but the splashing was not so loud as to drown what was being said.

Joshua peered in. The scene was

much as he'd expected, except in one particular.

Seven men and one woman were in the high-roofed shed. They were dwarfed by the twenty-five-foot height of the mining apparatus. Except for a couple of Skann's roughnecks, Joshua could put names to all of them.

Cord Skann, big, unshaven, dirty, a black cigarette burning between his fingers, was seated on the edge of an opened guard rail in front of the towering stamp mill. He ran a hand through his straggly hair, rubbed his big nose and regarded his prisoners with hot, gloating eyes.

A lantern among litter on a battered desk shed a yellow light that struggled to disperse the shed's gloom, throwing huge and misshapen shadows on the high walls and raftered roof.

The gang had unearthed a forgotten drum of oil and had poured the contents liberally over the sluggish moving parts of the rusted machinery. Splashes and puddles were everywhere.

The dripping, half-empty drum was on its side.

Jennie Bennett was tied to the only chair, her pretty face drawn, the colour of ashes and filled with terror.

The man who'd been introduced to Joshua as Joseph Darcy, but was Jennie's husband, the wealthy mines investor Ryan Bennett, was similarly trussed up and set down on an upended crate.

The one item in the tableau that came as a surprise to Joshua was the corpse.

It was of the missing town marshal, Charley Broadstreet, and was lying on a tarp Joshua had last seen wrapped around the bundle in the tray of the Bennetts' buckboard.

Click, click . . . the mental pieces slotted together. The Bennetts' odd visit to the abandoned mine was explained. Where better to dispose of an embarrassing body?

Joshua remembered, too, how he'd witnessed at the Silverville stage station the unexpected departure of the maid Maria, suddenly and generously paid off by 'Mr Darcy' and destined for faraway El Paso. Out of questioning or gossiping's way . . .

It seemed the Bennetts killed the marshal! But why?

He listened and learned.

' — and I figure you, Darcy, not only killed Charley Broadstreet in cold blood, you murdered my brother Zach, too,' Skann was saying, 'even though he'd done you a favour by executing this madam's stinkin' rat of a husband, the ex-Pink Rye Bennett.'

'That's a rotten lie!' Jennie burst out. 'Marshal Broadstreet wasn't murdered. He turned rogue lawman. He criminally assaulted me and drew his gun first — when he was caught in the act!'

Joshua noted that she made, of course, no attempt to correct Cord Skann's misapprehension about the male captive's identity. To do that — to reveal he was the Skann brothers' sworn enemy still alive — would make his death all the more certain.

'Yeah?' Skann jeered. 'An' so you had to come here to throw the body down a deep, disused mine shaft. Huh! That don't sound like a pair of wronged innocents to me! Sounds like you was hidin' some-thin', jest like you done afore.'

Bennett broke his red-faced silence.

'Jennie's telling the truth, man! Broadstreet dishonoured her — swear to God! She's done you no harm. Let her go! I beg it of you.'

Skann laughed at his pleading. He flipped away the butt of his cigarette, took out a fresh one and lit it with cat-and-mouse deliberation.

'Nope! You're both gonna die fer whatever you did to Zach, but it won't be ladies first. You'll go first, Darcy, an' the pretty li'l lovin' widow'll be made to watch fer her sins. It'll be messy, bloody, prob'ly painful. Mebbe you'll scream fer her, till your head's busted, or you're too broken up to draw breath. But no nevermind, the boys'll be hankerin' to give Goldilocks their comfort afterward.'

'What are you going to do, you filthy swine?'

'Why, you bein' so smart, lover boy, I reckon you shoulda guessed. We'll put you in the stamp mill. Crush you to bloody pulp! Ain't that a dandy idea? An' seein' as you won't be around to see your slut take her turn, we'll let you watch a dummy run . . . '

He gestured at Broadstreet's stiff body. 'Huck, throw the dead 'un into the mill! Bud, throw the lever an' start the beast up ag'in!'

15

Clouds of Sorrow Depart

Joshua bided his time to intervene. Surreptitiously, he glimpsed them shove Broadstreet's body in under the poised stamps. He heard the clanking mechanism come for a second time to resurrected life, flinging out dripped accumulations of excess oil from its recesses.

Jennie Bennett gave a small cry as the ponderous stamps thudded down on the corpse.

The thumps were muffled at first, but the mass was squashed after a few moments into a heap of red-stained rags around a soggy core. Quickly after, the mill's grim load broke up with a hideous crunching.

Joshua noticed a knothole in the shed's plank wall that would afford him safer observation and quietly shifted to it. He also broke open his Peacemaker and slipped a shell into the sixth, empty chamber.

When he resumed his spying, bits of flattened debris were clinging stickily to the rising stamps. Some splattered on to the shed floor.

Skann's grinning toughs whooped.

Bennett set his jaw and looked stoic, betraying no emotion except disgust.

Jennie tried to look away, but the man called Flip gripped her blonde head between strong, calloused hands, and wrenched it back, forcing her to face the frightening demonstration.

He growled words in her ear that Joshua couldn't catch but knew must be some awful threat he'd carry out if she didn't open her eyes.

Skann himself exulted at the success of the diabolical scheme. Broadstreet's body was crushed to little more than lumps and smears. The clanking, thumping and vibrating was halted. The close, oil-tinged atmosphere of the place was supplanted by the over-sweet, sanguine smell of a slaughterhouse.

'It's you next, Darcy,' he told Bennett. 'Then Rye Bennett's woman!' He was leering, mocking. 'That'll be after a spell o' that *dishonourin'* I figure her taste is apt to run to!'

He turned to Jennie. 'How's that, bitch? A husband whose head was blown off, then two studs fed to an ore crusher!'

'You fiend!' she gasped.

'You ain't no angel yourself, woman. A sharin' of your gutter ways with the boys, then you go to the crusher an' join your three beaus in hell!'

But Huck, impatient to have his share of the fooling he'd missed with their last woman captive, wanted to rearrange the order of Skann's plan.

'I say we deal with the brazen hussy first. Straight off! That way, Darcy can watch as extry punishment afore he goes under the stamps.'

Skann bristled at the questioning of his authority.

'I'm the boss, ain't I? I said we git shut of Darcy first, then you can take your turn of the fun. Weren't that plain?'

'Listen,' Huck came back, 'yuh don't have to take it hard, Cord. It's jest a switcharound. Why don't we take a vote on it?'

Tension rose in the air. The outlaws all looked at the arguing pair and at one another.

Outnumbered as he was, Joshua decided the time would never be riper.

He sprang into the open doorway, fully aware that his desperate gamble could miscarry with tragic results. For death stood before him and he was risking Jennie and Ryan Bennett's threatened lives as well as his own.

Jennie screamed.

Joshua's Peacemaker bucked against his wrist and boomed shatteringly. A surprised outlaw looked stunned as a bullet smashed into his belly. He was flung backward by the lead's impact almost into the crusher. Blood spurted from him.

The rest of the Skann bunch instinctively scattered, grabbing for their guns. Joshua's Peacemaker roared again and another man fell, half his face severely, redly damaged.

Joshua's fire was returned, but he was unharmed and shot a third outlaw in his retreating back without compunction.

The Bennetts stared incredulously at the scene of battle and death that had developed so rapidly before them.

Three of their captors had fallen to Joshua's smoking gun, but that left another three still on their feet. One of them was Cord Skann, who dived behind the cover of the mill's solid framework, tilting his revolver in its holster and firing through the slit bottom.

A thrill of joy ran through Joshua when the crouching gang boss's hasty shot accidentally took out Huck. The man doubled up, dropping his gun in the act of drawing it, and clutched his belly. He crumpled, in screeching agony, to the floor, the blood jetting through his clasping fingers.

Just Skann and one other — Bud, Joshua thought it was — to best; and so far just a couple of misaimed shots fired at him in return.

But Joshua couldn't count on more luck. Together, Skann and Bud could have him bracketed. And more stray shots could easily kill either Jennie or Ryan Bennett, turning his rescue bid into a futile failure.

With three bullets left, Joshua drew a careful bead on the lantern on the desk and shot out its light in an explosion of glass and metal fragments.

Now it was two shots left, and two opponents facing him, seeking him out in the shadows of the shed.

'No one's that fast, that good a marksman,' Skann said, fighting his own doubts. 'We'll get 'im, Bud!'

Joshua moved forward into the gloom, away from the slanting grey light through the door, feinting in one direction yet taking another. He felt sweat trickling down his spine, caught a hint of movement from where he'd last seen Bud . . . a blur of darker, shifting shadow.

He reacted by pure instinct. He twisted, turned and triggered as Bud fired at him. But his own snapped shot failed to hit Bud and the flare from his gun's muzzle pinpointed him for Skann.

'I got you now, Dillard, you sonofabitch!'

Damn it! Joshua thought for a moment he had lost — a hasty shot from the crowing Skann whanged past his face so close he felt its heat.

Then, all at once, came a development truly worthy of Ryan Bennett's 'always expect the unexpected'.

Hot fragments of the shot-out lantern had been quietly resting, smouldering, in the litter atop the battered old desk which had soaked up the spilled lamp oil.

Joshua gasped as they flared up. In split seconds the desk itself was ablaze.

Then the flames leaped, flashing over like small wildfires into the puddles and rivulets of the oil Skann's men had thrown on the stamp mill.

Skann was evidently as shocked into immobility as Joshua.

Bud, who had been closest to the desk, screamed and ran out on to the open floor, his pants' legs afire.

As he passed the toppled oil drum, beating at his clothing, flying bits of ash and flame transferred themselves to it. The container blew up in a *whumph* that produced a wall of flame and oily black smoke across the shed.

Joshua's senses reeled.

No longer could he see a target for his last bullet. He was cut off from the mill, Skann and Bud, and it might be only moments before the whole shed went up in a fireball.

He pushed his gun into his belt and pulled out a trusty and treasured clasp-knife. It had his name engraved on it in elegant, flowing script and was a gift from his late wife.

Offering up a prayer of thanks in her name and memory, and for the life and safety of the Bennetts, he flung himself to the prisoners' side. The heat of the fire was so close to them, he felt his hair singeing.

He turned his first attention to severing the bonds at Bennett's feet with his knife.

'No! Save my wife!' Bennett cried.

'The door! Go!' Joshua blurted back. 'I'll carry Mrs Bennett!'

Then he picked up both Jennie Bennett and the chair she was tied to as one item and stumbled away from the choking inferno.

They escaped not a second too soon.

The beams of the towering stamp mill, engulfed by the fire, gave way and the structure collapsed in on its solid foundations. The shed walls folded in on the swirling dust, the smoke and the glowing debris.

Joshua thought he heard a thin, impossibly shrill scream of terror. But the utterance was brief, lost in the roar of the restoked fire.

They staggered up a dirt track away from the Maybelline's workings. When they paused to look back, and for Joshua to cut Skann's former prisoners fully free, they saw a dense cloud of black smoke hanging over the buildings.

Exhausted, they sat and watched. The flames went higher and higher as structure after structure took fire.

Joshua said, 'I think you've seen the last of your Maybelline No. 1, Mr Bennett . . . and your old enemies.'

'Thank God,' Jennie said.

★ ★ ★

For the next week, Joshua Dillard and Flora Bennett were guests of her brother and sister-in-law in their house at Silverville. Poverty Joe — the real Joseph Darcy — was also a guest, patched up by Doc Pike and expected to make a steady recovery.

Joshua knew it was time for him to be moving on. The need was pressing to seek paying opportunities for him to use his unorthodox detectiving talents. He was, of course, collecting no big commission from Flora's unforthcoming inheritance under the terms of Ryan Bennett's 'lost' will. So he would be riding out with empty pockets, like he always did.

But it amused him to dally and enjoy Flora's pleasure in getting to know again the brother who'd 'returned from the dead', plus his charming wife.

The grand Bennett mansion offered plenty of guest accommodation. Joshua was thus given an uncommon and generous chance for privacy and rest.

Late in the evening before he was set to leave, a soft tapping on the door of Joshua's room announced that both were about to be interrupted.

Downstairs, in the front parlour, the piano was being played and voices murmured companionably: Jennie's, Rye's, Joe's.

He sat up in bed and called, 'Come in.'

Somehow, he wasn't surprised to see Flora.

He was surprised, just mildly, to see she wore only a thin white nightgown under a prettily embroidered shawl that concealed little.

She came and sat on his bed.

'You can't have made any money from my case, Joshua,' she said in frank, vibrant tones. 'But there's something else I promised that I want to deliver before you go. I haven't forgotten, and I *must* and *will* do it . . . As a woman of her word.'

The vestiges of Joshua's tranquillity fled, but to pretend reluctance he didn't feel would be insulting. He let his gaze rove over her, and saw the beauty of a determined, desirable woman. She still had the airs and graces of the fine — but reserved — lady he'd met in Denver. Jennie and Ryan might soon be casting her in the role of a maiden aunt, too, if he didn't miss his guess. Yet she was way too complex to stereotype.

Her features still had that delicacy

which is supposed to indicate breeding; her hazel eyes and the arch of her eyebrows showed cool appraisal as she surveyed his bare chest. But there were also dimples of mischief at the corners of the mouth that redeemed her classical severity.

And it was the real measure of the steel in Flora Bennett's character that despite her recent experiences in an unfamiliar and ugly world, she had no apprehension, no unwillingness to meet the commitment she'd made. In fact, she seemed to view the situation as a little humorous.

She dropped her shawl and swung her legs up on to the bed. They were long and shapely legs, as Joshua had known they would be.

His heart beat faster. Such behaviour broke all the rules of the hypocritical establishment to which she belonged, he thought . . . but the shackles of those be damned!

Later, he asked tentatively, 'Don't you feel this might be a mistake?'

'Hush, Joshua!' she replied shakily. 'How could anything so pleasurable be bad? I've found out Heaven really can be just a small sin away, but tomorrow it will be over the horizon.'

In due course, they laid back to listen to the soothing sounds of Jennie's singing downstairs.

Beautiful dreamer, out on the sea
Mermaids are chaunting the wild lorelie;
Over the streamlet vapours are borne,
Waiting to fade at the bright coming morn.
Beautiful dreamer, beam on my heart,
E'en as the morn on the streamlet and sea:
Then will all clouds of sorrow depart,
Beautiful dreamer, awake unto me!
Beautiful dreamer, awake unto me!

Flora sighed.

'Jennie's beautiful dream — her life with Ryan — carries on. As it turned out, it hadn't really been broken, had it? For them, the dream will *never* end!'

Joshua knew what she was saying. Their realized dream was beautiful, too; it was sweet and exciting and surely would prove memorable.

For now, he had the night and Flora. But when the sun rose tomorrow, they both understood their time together would be over.

THE END

We do hope that you have enjoyed reading this large print book.

Did you know that all of our titles are available for purchase?

We publish a wide range of high quality large print books including:
**Romances, Mysteries, Classics
General Fiction
Non Fiction and Westerns**

Special interest titles available in large print are:
**The Little Oxford Dictionary
Music Book, Song Book
Hymn Book, Service Book**

Also available from us courtesy of Oxford University Press:
**Young Readers' Dictionary
(large print edition)
Young Readers' Thesaurus
(large print edition)**

For further information or a free brochure, please contact us at:
**Ulverscroft Large Print Books Ltd.,
The Green, Bradgate Road, Anstey,
Leicester, LE7 7FU, England.
Tel:** (00 44) **0116 236 4325
Fax:** (00 44) **0116 234 0205**